KEEP CALM
AND
KILL
YOUR
WIFE

LUCKY STEVENS

Published by Waters and Baxter

Copyright © 2014, 2020, 2024 by Lucky Stevens

ISBN-13: 979-8-9897034-1-8

Printed in the United States of America.

For Baby

ACKNOWLEDGMENTS

I would like to sincerely acknowledge and thank those who have truly helped to make this book what it is. It's funny when I look back at what I thought was a completed manuscript and after having gotten such wonderful suggestions, feedback and insight, realize how much better this labor of love now is because of the generosity of others. Thank you all so much for your willingness to be honest with me and for your help in letting me see my work through different eyes. Thank you to Mom, Dad, Bro, Vijay, the Mill City Press gang and, of course, Summer Knight.

I would also like to thank Spell Check for consistently pointing out my spelling errors. I must say that I put in some pretty long hours—sometimes late into the night—but your relentless commitment never wavered throughout the writing of my book. Not only are you thorough, but your feedback is given with such decorum, subtlety and finesse that I never for a minute felt attacked or belittled in any way. This won't mean anything to others, of course, but thanks for the "little red wavy lines".

"Repeat after me. With this ring…"

"With this ring…"

"I thee wed."

"I thee wed."

"By the power vested in me by the state of California, I now pronounce you, husband and wife. You may kill the bride. I mean kiss the bride."

His head went driving forward as he sat upright. He was sweating and breathing hard, the covers bunched around his mid-section.

His wife turned over and faced him. "What's the matter, Honey? Did you have a nightmare?" She rubbed his arm.

He turned his head in her direction. "You know what they say about nightmares don't you?"

"No."

"It's only a nightmare if you let it bother you."

ONE

HART WAS DOING ABOUT fifty when the little Japanese job came out of nowhere and cut him off. He layed on his horn and constructed a pretty nice little string of expletives that, in spite of the content, rolled off his tongue with a certain polished eloquence.

The car, a bare bones Toyota Tercel, was now in front of his semi and seemed to be making no effort whatsoever to compensate for the cutoff. As a matter of fact it was chugging along a good fifteen miles per hour below the speed limit.

Hart rolled his eyes and punched the horn again. "Come on. First you cut me off and then you drag your ass down my lane, you stupid idiot," he shouted.

The road ran along a desolate strip of warehouse-sized businesses. Strictly industrial with only one lane for coming and going.

And if all this wasn't bad enough, now the driver of the Tercel was sticking her arm out the window and pointing above the car's roof for Hart to pull over.

"Pull over? Just get the hell out of my way."

The shoulder, when there was one, was nothing more than a sliver of dirt. The Tercel then pulled over, the ass of the car stuck out, making it that much harder to pass.

Hart wanted to just go around her. And he would have loved to have clipped her bumper in the process. Instead, out of angry and bored curiosity, he pulled over as well, hugging the sliver of shoulder as much as he could.

Hart got out of his cab and slammed the door. He was fuming, but also scoffing in pure disbelief. *What the hell could possibly be going on here?*

He rounded the cab of his truck and stopped. Standing in front of him was a woman. She was half turned toward him, her hands on her hips and her silky blonde hair was covering the left side of her face.

The view took over for a moment as he put his impulsive mouth on hold, his eyes tracing her silhouette up and down a few times. She was wearing a body-hugging red dress, slitted up the side, and high heels— who knew what kind? They made her legs look great.

But the thing that really knocked Hart out was what was *not* there. It was a button right across the juicy part of the bust line on her dress. *Oh my God.* You've heard the expression, 'Take a picture, why don't you.' ? Well Hart stopped dead in his tracks. He wanted to take a picture alright. Then he wanted to blow it up and stare at it all day long…

That little gap there. It drove him nuts. When his eyes traced her body up and down, he couldn't wait to get back to that part. Huge red bursting plums on the outside and the same luscious contours on the inside, half white and lacy, gently scooping, and half rosy succulent flesh that would never be riper.

As he stared at her, for the life of him, he couldn't remember what he had been mad about. And if he could, maybe he didn't care anymore.

She was the first to talk. "What are you doing?"

"What do you mean what am I doing? You cut me off." He said it matter-of-factly, his tone in check, unsure at this point exactly how he wanted to come off.

And as the conversation progressed, Hart's eyes dropped to that incredible gap in her dress every chance he could, as he tried not to appear too obvious. It was something that he had absolutely no talent for whatsoever. As a result, he looked *incredibly* obvious and she noticed every time.

The conversation, other than Hart's view, was going nowhere, that is until the woman pointed her finger at him and began waving it. Her mouth opened, hanging in mid-air until she finally spoke.

"Wait a minute. Wait a minute. Hart?"

Hearing her say his name felt exciting. *She knows me?* And then, the next moment, terrifying. *What or where does she know me from?*

"Maybe. Who wants to kn—" And then it hit him as he really looked at her face for the first time. It wasn't that it didn't knock him out. It did. It's just that there had been so much to focus on.

He squinted a little and pointed back to her. "Brandy." He kept pointing, moving his finger up and down. "Wow, you look incredible."

She smiled. "Thanks."

"Now your driving, that could use some work."

"Maybe you could give me some pointers sometime. You a good driver, Hart?"

Before he could answer, a woman walked by, slowing but not stopping as she said, "You missed a button." She sort of whispered it as if Hart wouldn't hear and she winced a little like she was embarrassed.

"Mind your own business," said Brandy.

The woman glanced back and frowned and then kept on walking.

Maybe the missed button was on purpose.

Hell, maybe this whole meeting had been on purpose.

———————————

The small indentation in the wall was like a bullseye as the door to Brandy's apartment flung open and the knob slammed into it making a fresh gaping hole in the plaster. Hart and Brandy couldn't get their clothes off fast enough as they pawed and tugged at each other like a couple of animals. They were nowhere near the stage where anything mattered other than getting at each other and fast. Everything else came a distant second. Ripped clothes, birth control, damaged plaster, bumps, bruises, scratches.

When they were done, they lay on top of one another heaving unevenly, and eventually in rhythm. Then they talked and ate pizza in bed. It was all just passing time until the next round.

"So how long's it been since I last saw you?" Hart asked.

"The wedding."

"Really, that long? That's ten years. Boy, you sure have grown up and in all the right places, too."

Brandy smiled. "You know I always had a crush on you."

"Yeah? No, I didn't know that." It felt great to be the object of desire by someone so beautiful.

"Yeah, yeah. Think about it. I mean there you were, star of the football team. Three years older than me and then you started dating my cousin. I loved rooting you on. And you didn't even know I existed."

"I do now."

"So how is Summer?"

"She's alright."

"And how's your life? Are you happy?"

He shrugged. "It's okay. You know, making a living. Doing what I have to do."

They were quiet for a moment, both thinking. "You know," Hart continued. "It's funny. When you're in high school you think your life's going to turn out so much different than it actually does."

"What did you think it was going to be like?"

"I thought I'd be a star running back in the NFL and stinking rich."

Brandy smiled. "You were amazing to watch. You had such, such—"

"Dramatic flair."

"That's it, dramatic flair. Great way to put it. I still remember how you'd spin around, avoid tackles and the way you'd run. Oh, it was amazing."

"Those were great times," he said.

"Do you ever wish your life could be different?"

"Yeah, I guess everyone does sometimes. Do you?"

"Oh yeah. So what do you think separates people who wish things were different from people who make them different?" she asked.

"Balls. Determination. What do you wish was different with you?"

"A lot of things. I wish I had someone to share my life with."

Then she told him about her husband who died a few years ago and asked him if he remembered the last time they were supposed to see each other.

"Supposed to?"

"Yeah. It was supposed to be two years ago at the reading of my grandmother's will, but I never showed up. I already knew what was going to happen. How Summer was going to get her cabin and all. Summer didn't even like that place."

"You got some money."

Brandy pushed her lips together. "Yeah. That's all gone now."

She smiled wanly and looked Hart in the eyes. "I guess I have a lot to be jealous about when it comes to Summer."

Then they started up again, grinding and clawing at each other until they could barely walk.

TWO

HIS SNAPPING FINGERS went completely unnoticed. The busy waitress, whose flared skirt twirled like a spinning umbrella as she bounced from table to table like a pinball, was just trying to keep up. "Well, there's another couple percent off her tip."

"Oh Hart, you can eat a couple a fries without ketchup. It won't kill you. Jeez."

"Actually, French fries can kill you. Four out of five surgeon generals'll tell you that."

"Oh, shut up." Brandy talked while powdering her nose. "You know, you haven't even complimented me on my new hairstyle yet."

"Well you should have said something about your hair. I'd be happy to compliment you."

"Well?" she said.

"Well what?"

Brandy clenched her lips and pointed to her hair. "Oh yeah, it looks great, Baby."

She sighed. "I guess it's that two month itch. You don't notice me anymore."

"Of course I notice you." Hart looked around and snapped his fingers again at the waitress's backside which was a good ten feet away. "It's just that I got a lot of stuff on my mind."

"Like what?"

"Like my wife, for one."

"Oh her. What about her?" Brandy rested her chin on the heel of her hand.

"I'm just tired of her. She has no dr—"

"—dramatic flair," interrupted Brandy. "Yes, I've

heard that from you once or twice. And by once or twice, I mean a few hundred times."

Hart smiled. "Now, see you have dramatic flair. And by dramatic flair, I mean you're a bitch."

Brandy fluffed her hair. "Well, why don't you just—" She stopped.

"Yeah?"

"Oh never mind. I was going to suggest that you get a divorce, but that'll never happen. We've had that discussion once or twice as well."

"Well hey, it's not easy. Divorce has its problems. Like giving up half my stuff."

"Well, I guess that leaves you no choice."

"Exactly."

"You're going to have to kill her." She drank her Coke, keeping one eye on Hart.

"What?" Hart said a little too loudly. Then leaning in, "You want me to kill my wife? Your cousin? You're crazy." Hart laughed.

"Yeah, I didn't think you'd have the onions."

Hart's head turned as his peripheral vision, and then his hand, caught the waitress as she was on the verge of whizzing by. Squeezing her arm, his face stretched into a wide frozen grin. "Can I have some fuckin' ketchup, please?"

The waitress frowned and started to open her mouth, unable to say anything, as she reached into her apron and handed him a bottle.

Hart threw her a perfunctory "thanks" and turned back to Brandy.

"Anyway, are you serious about Summer? It's not exactly like taking out the trash, you know."

"Okay, forget it. Drive a truck for the rest of your life. Stay poor. Stay married—to *her*. Go ahead."

Hart clenched his teeth. "You know you're painting a pretty nice picture here, but I'd still have to drive a truck, you know. I'd still be poor. It's not like Summer's got any money."

"Not on her, no. But remember most people are worth more dead than alive," Brandy said.

Hart looked at her.

Brandy put her hands out and held his across the table. She cocked her head just so, and her hair fell over her eye, Veronica Lake-style. "I'm sorry, Baby. I didn't mean to upset you. We don't have to talk about it anymore."

"It's okay." Hart looked down. "It's just that, I don't know, I really want to do something with my life. I mean I've worked my ass off driving that truck for ten years and all I've got to show for it is a mortgaged house, an aching back and a pack of hemorrhoids."

"So it sounds like you're saying that you really have nothing to lose."

"I think I got married too young."

"It was right out of high school, right?"

"Yeah. It's crazy when you think about it. I mean I never really had a chance to figure things out. She's basically the only girl I've ever been with and I never really knew what else was out there. What else I was missing. Like you."

Brandy looked at Hart. She smiled and it spoke volumes. Sexy. Positive. Devilish.

"And I had to go to work right away to support us. I mean who knows what I could have accomplished if I hadn't married Summer."

"Sounds to me like you're in a dead end."

"Thanks for rubbing it in."

Brandy shook her head. "I'm not trying to rub it in. I'm trying to say there's hope. But you got to get Summer out of the way. It's the only option if you really want to solve all your problems."

Hart looked at her. She really was beautiful. "Don't worry," she continued. "I'll plan it out with you. It's the only way. You gotta decide. Do you want to be happy or live some dull existence?"

She let it sink in a moment before adding, "And do want your happiness to start now? Or do you just want to dream about it? Let everyone else be rich and happy?"

Hart stared into Brandy's eyes for a long time. "How would we do it?"

THREE

ART PULLED UP TO 106 N. Hudson Road and parked his '11 Acura TSX in the cracked driveway in front of his house right next to Summer's eight-year-old Hyundai Santa Fe. He looked at the older vehicle and frowned. *No dramatic flair whatsoever*, he thought.

He had been working extra hours of late but had nothing to show for it as his "overtime" was little more than a ruse directed at his wife in order to spend more time with Brandy. In short, his supposed new found work ethic was doing nothing to pay down his gambling debts. But no matter, he assured himself—he would soon be rolling in extra cash.

His wife, Summer, had also been keeping herself busy with extracurricular activities of some sort. Hart didn't think it was an affair, and didn't particularly care one way or the other.

As Hart strolled up the path to the front door, he, once again, completely missed the beautiful new stargazer lilies which Summer had recently planted adjacent to the walk.

"Honey, I'm home," he called out, looking at the local paper he had just retrieved from the porch. No sooner had he shut the door behind him than he felt the paper being swatted from his hand with one fist as another came flying toward his face. He tilted his head, which was unnecessary, as the punch was clearly pulled. In the meantime, the newspaper and all its circulars scattered to the floor.

"Hi-YA!" she screamed.

Hart's mind quickly groped for order and he held his thumb with a wincing look on his face, a scowl born of irritation and surprise rather than pain.

"Summer? What the hell's going on?"

"Oh Sweetheart, I'm sorry," Summer said. "Are you okay?"

Hart looked annoyed as he shook his thumb. "I'm fine, but what the hell are you doing?"

Summer bent down and picked up the paper. "Just what you told me to do. Trying to be more dramatic."

"I said dramatic *flair*. And you can't manufacture it. You either got it or you don't."

"You're the one who told me to surprise you with unexpected attacks when I started taking karate. You said I would never be able to catch you off guard."

"Well the only reason you caught me off guard is that I wasn't ready for it," Hart said.

Summer was half-amused and opened her mouth to reply. Only she didn't talk fast enough.

"Besides, I don't remember that conversation," he continued. "It doesn't sound like something I'd even say."

"Well, I'm sorry Sweetheart. Are you okay?"

"I didn't even know you were taking karate."

Summer shrugged, not wanting to argue. "Well, I did tell you. It was right around the time you told me to surprise you with unexpected attacks." A joking gleam filled her eyes.

Hart threw his hands up. Then he bit his bottom lip and forced himself to lower the volume. "So, how about if we take a little walk, Honey?"

Summer was a little tired but readily agreed as they rarely did things like that. "Just let me get my coat." She walked toward the bedroom, just a few feet away from the foray. "So how was your day?"

"Fine," said Hart, flipping through the newspaper. "Aren't you going to ask me about my karate class?" Summer asked, calling from the bedroom. "I think I get the idea."

The neighborhood was pleasant enough. Mid-century tract homes dotted the winding streets and most people kept them in reasonably good shape. It was a nice backdrop as they held hands strolling at a relatively slow pace.

"Did you notice the lilies I planted?" Summer asked.

"Beautiful," he said looking down at her, smiling.

She smiled back. They continued walking in silence for a moment, the cool night air grazing their faces. Hart sneaked a peek at his watch and they began to suddenly speak at the same time.

"You first," he said.

"Thanks. I just wanted to tell you I've been thinking about taking flying lessons."

"Huh. Sounds expensive."

"A little, but I'll be honest, with you working so much overtime, I really need to keep busy and it's something I've always wanted to do."

"Huh. That's kind of surprising considering you're afraid of your own shadow."

"That's exactly why I want to do it." Hart nodded. "Okay, my turn."

"Okay."

"Well, I've been doing a lot of thinking, and I really think you're right. I think we should have a kid."

Summer's mouth opened and froze for a moment. "Really?"

"I'm not kidding. I'm really ready now."

Tears glazed over Summer's eyes. "Oh my God, I can't believe this," she said, leaping into his arms. And then she slowly peeled herself away, thinking it may be too good to be true. "Are you sure this is what you want?"

"I'm sure," he said as they embraced again.

"This is so wonderful," she said, and then began giggling through her tears. "And just think, now the Smith name will live on."

"Hey you know what?" Hart said, in between slurpy bites of cereal.

Summer was sitting down, arranging her vitamins in a perfect row. "What?" she said.

"I just thought of something. You better hold off on those flying lessons."

"Why? You can fly if you're pregnant."

"No, it's not that. We need to get life insurance now that we're going to be parents. And they're going to ask about dangerous hobbies, so you're just going to have to wait until we're approved."

"I'm not even pregnant yet."

"Don't worry Honey, we'll work on that."

"Oooh, I'm so excited," she said, scuffling over to where Hart was sitting and embracing him from behind. "Hey listen, seriously, it can take awhile to get pregnant. Let's hold off on insurance and save the premiums until we really need it."

"Forget it. I don't want to wait," Hart said sharply and louder than he wanted to.

Summer let go. "What's the matter?"

"Nothing, nothing. I'm sorry. I just feel strongly about this."

Summer went back and sat down.

"It's just that it can take a while to get approved, that's all," said Hart. He walked over behind her chair and put his hands on her shoulders. "I'm sorry. Hey look at this way, the faster you're approved for insurance, the faster you can start taking flying lessons. I'll even help you pay for them."

"Okay," she said softly, smiling as he kissed her cheek.

FOUR

BRANDY'S APARTMENT building was a couple of towns over from Summer and Hart's house.

The outside was cold and thoroughly lacking in charm, having been stuccoed over and outfitted with vinyl framed windows sitting in walls without sills or shutters. The one advantage was that it was courtyard style. No one shared walls, each unit being its own self- contained structure. It worked out well and had been their regular tryst spot since that first time a few months back.

Hart and Brandy lay naked together under the covers. Her head was propped up on his rising and falling chest, while her fingers traced circles in his ample tufts of hair lying just below her resting chin.

She let their rapid breathing die down before she spoke. "So tell me what's happening. How are things going?"

Hart smiled. "Well, it was funny at work today when I was dropping off a load of gravel, over at Pacific, Joe told me a great story."

"Not that," she said. "I'm talking about with Summer."

"Oh, oh. Things are going good. We were approved for life insurance, both of us, last week."

"Were you able to get a million?"

"Piece of cake. Once we mentioned kids, no problem. Those premiums are little steep though. Maybe I should cancel mine soon."

"Forget it," Brandy said, bunching up her face. "You're not going to be paying for very long. Besides, don't draw any attention to yourself. That's stupid."

"Yeah, I guess. Let's see, what else? Um, she's not pregnant, so that's good. I put a pill in her orange juice every morning like you said. One time she knocked over the glass after drinking only half of it. You know what a klutz she can be. Oh, and one time I forgot to slip her one."

"Well be careful."

"Tell me about it. She said she was ovulating that day and she wanted to—ow!"

Brandy lifted her arm and frittered away three chest hairs she had just yanked out.

"Son of a bitch! What'd you do that for?"

"The same reason you were going to tell me about your wife—I'm thoughtless."

"Yeah, I guess I can be a little thoughtless."
And with that, Hart wiggled back, curled up and
catapulted Brandy out of bed with his feet.

Before she even hit the floor, she began hurling
a series of obscenities toward him.

Hart laughed. "Hey don't blame me. I'm
thoughtless."

Brandy wasn't amused and came tearing at him
with fists clenched. She jumped on top of him, arms
flailing. Hart just laughed as he grabbed her wrists
and flipped her over. On top of her now, they
slapped and poked at each other until the absurdity
of it all became almost conspicuous. By then they
both were laughing so hard they could barely
breathe.

"You jerk," Brandy said, with a half-hearted
swipe, calming down.

"You tart," he said as he attacked her neck with
his lips. It only took moments from there before
they were in a full embrace, their bodies intertwined
in inexorable desire.

The desk, despite the mounds of work, was
ridiculously organized. Summer was pounding away
on her computer keyboard with an almost
imperceptible grin on her face. The only thing that
occasionally interrupted her, besides her colleagues,
was the slight fluttering of her fingers above the
keys that would occur every half page or so. It was
a little habit that she had developed when she had
first learned to type back in junior high. "Just learn

how to type, Summer," her mother used to tell her, "and you'll never be out of a job."

"Summer, could I get the Dockweiler and Hassett files, please?"

Summer stopped typing. "No problem, Mr. Day. Do you want me to bring them to you?"

Robert Day had recently become a partner at the law firm of Grimley, Lockwood and Shapiro. He was 6'2", had a full head of dark wavy hair, piercing blue eyes and a killer smile. But what really drew people to him was the fact that he didn't act at all like he possessed the above credentials.

"Nah, I'll save you the trip. It never takes you longer than ten seconds to find anything anyway. And Summer, please don't call me Mr. Day. It makes me feel like I'm seventy."

"Sorry. Old habits die hard." It was half-true and half-not. Sometimes she just called him "Mister" to tease him.

Summer smiled and leapt into action. Like most of the women at the law firm, Summer harbored a secret crush on Bob. And in her case, it actually had some merit. Early on in her employment at Grimley, Bob had asked her out, which was something he rarely did at the office. Already in love with Hart and just weeks away from getting engaged, she had politely turned him down. "Here you go, Bob, Dockweiler" said Summer, handing him the first file. "And Hassett."

"What took you so long?" asked Bob, smiling.

Summer laughed and after a beat said, "Did you need anything else?"

Bob had to consciously break his gaze. "No, no, this is good. Thank you."

"Anytime."

Bob patted the files, turned and walked away. "You're amazing, Summer." Then he cringed to himself. *That sounded awkward.*

Summer immediately hit the keyboard again as Joanna came swooping in.

"I swear Summer, you're the only one in the office

that can turn that man's legs to jelly," Joanna whispered with a huge grin.

Summer smiled uncomfortably and then scoffed, "You always say that."

"Because it's true. Come on, girl, let's take a break. It's 10:30."

The courtyard of the office complex was large and it struck a pleasant balance between its hardscape and softscape. Giant boulders suggested a solid permanence, while ferns of different varieties infused the grounds with a lush sense of vitality. The paths were comfortably wide, yet small enough that they furnished a certain intimacy and structure. A large fountain in the middle, provided beauty and a perfect, tranquil soundtrack.

It was the ideal place to get away from things, and the one that Summer and Joanna usually picked when they had the chance to take their breaks together.

Joanna lit up a cigarette, careful to blow the smoke away from Summer, as the two women walked at a leisurely pace down the arcing path.

"So tell me what's been going on. You look really happy lately."

Summer smiled. "I really am, Joanna. Things are just going so great lately."

"It shows. Hey, are you pregnant?" She moved her cigarette a little behind her.

"No not yet. It's only been a few months. But I'm really not stressed about it. It'll happen."

"Absolutely," said Joanna.

"No, it's just everything. Hart and I have been getting along so well lately, ever since we decided to have kids."

"Yeah, yeah, that can really change a man."

"Yeah, I guess so. I think we were in kind of a rut for a while but lately he's been so sweet, like when we were first married. And I love the classes I've been taking. The flying lessons are incredible."

"Have you actually been up in the air yet?"

"Yeah, it's amazing. I honestly never thought I could do it. It scares the hell out of me, but it's just incredible."

"Wow, I don't know if I could do that."

"Nah, I don't think you could either. No way."

Joanna's face contorted. "What do you mean?" she asked, blowing smoke from the corner of her mouth.

Summer laughed. "I'm just kidding. Of course you could. I'm scared to death of flying. If I can do it, anyone could."

Joanna smiled and playfully nudged Summer with her shoulder.

"You know what's funny Joanna? When someone says they can't do something, it's fine. But when someone *else* says they can't, they get offended."

"I know *I* did."

They looked at each other and laughed.

"Hey Joanna, what do you want to be when you grow up?" Summer spied a translucent rock and picked it up.

"Rich. Why do you ask that?"

"I'm was just thinking, I love my job but I'm not sure I want to be a secretary my whole life, you know what I mean? I feel like a kid, like I can do anything. You know I might want to be a lawyer one day. Or a pilot."

"You *sound* like a kid."

"I mean, why not?"

"No reason. You're young."

"You know, I wish I could just take classes all day. When I was a kid, I don't think I really appreciated school. Now I'm loving my paralegal courses, karate, flying."

"Wow, I don't know where you get all your energy.

And you're going to be a mother?"

"I know, I should slow down," Summer said. Then she tossed her little rock and hopscotched ahead.

———————————

The air-conditioning in his truck was on the fritz. Not a good day for it either. Ninety-five degrees and he was sitting in a parking lot, otherwise known as the 57 Freeway. Maybe he'd call Brandy. He dug into his pocket and grasped the phone. One bar left. It was far from the first time. For some reason he could never remember to juice up his phone. Summer had even given him a charger that could be plugged into the cigarette lighter, but he had somehow managed to lose it.

Sweating profusely, he glanced over at the car sitting next to him which just happened to be his all-time favorite, an Acura NSX. From his vantage point he could only see the passenger—a beautiful red-head with a curvy figure. Her hair was blowing gently, no doubt from the frigid air-conditioning jetting out from the vents. He quickly decided that it made no difference at all what the

driver of the car looked like. With money, he could have that car and that girl no matter how ugly his mug might be. *Why does everyone have to have it better than me?*

So what else could Hartence Smith III do but look at the red-head sitting in *that* car while he listened to the radio?

After *Hotel California* ended, a lottery commercial came on. Hart scoffed. "You have to make your own luck in this world. I'm not waiting for some stupid lottery," he said out loud. That didn't stop him from buying a few tickets a week, however.

He looked to his left. It was her. The red-head. She had seen him talking to himself. He clenched his lips in an embarrassed smile while almost imperceptibly nodding. Then he got the bright idea to pretend he was singing along with the radio. She quickly turned away, her expression unchanged. God, she was beautiful.

"She probably thinks I was talking to myself," he said out loud, before deciding he better switch to thinking. He wiped the sweat off of his face and pulled his body forward, trying to get some air to his aching back. And then he just sat there for a moment before strangling the steering wheel, shaking his head back and forth and screaming, "I HATE THIS FUCKING JOB!" The red-head looked over at him again. That got her attention.

FIVE

"YEAH! YES-S-S! Look at that. It's fuckin' beautiful," Louie exclaimed as he reeled her in. She had to be at least a thirty pounder.

Hart whistled. "You are one lucky son of a bitch, you know that?"

"Nothing but skill, my man," said Louie.

"Oh, get over yourself," Hart said with a grin. "Just remember who gave you the bait."

Louie was one of Hart's oldest friends and they were each the best man at the other's wedding. In some ways they were so much alike it was kind of scary. And that fact was what seemed to keep them so close for all these years.

It was also what seemed to be at the core of an underlying animosity that both seemed to hold for the other. And one which had led to numerous tooth- loosening, drag-out brawls over the years, even as adults.

Ninety-nine percent of the time they could rib each other unmercifully and simply laugh it off—genuinely get a roaring kick out of it. But if either's mood was off just a little bit, or one went just an inch too far, it was Ali-Frazier all over again.

"Yeah, I'm sure every time I think back on this gorgeous hunk of bass, I'll think of you and your fuckin' dollar-fifty K-mart lure. That's going to be the primary part of my story, uh-huh."

Hart cracked open a beer and sat down on a fallen tree trunk. "You know, I never realized before what a fuckin' sarcastic son of a bitch you are. It's really an ugly side of you. Terrible, terrible."

"You know what the ugly side of you is, Hart? The outside. I don't know how Summer can take that mug of yours day after day."

Louie sat down next to Hart and grabbed his own beer.

"Well, beauty is in the eye of the beholder," said Hart as he casually stood and then purposely bent down and ripped a fart toward Louie's face.

"Oh Jeez," said Louie as he smiled and walked a few feet away.

Hart laughed. "There's a beauty for your eye to behold."

Darkness had blanketed the night sky, pocketing the sun and allowing other forms of illumination to peek out and dazzle those who took the time to delight in their brilliance. It takes a certain wisdom, or age, or attitude to appreciate such things. The moon and the stars and the fire which danced atop the twisty, sinewy logs, almost transparent in their hot red glow, played their parts magnificently that night. And they were there for the taking.

The fish was good, dissolving nicely in the stomachs of both men. In the middle of nowhere. Teeming with desolation. Hart looked at the trees and took in the quiet, interrupted only by crickets and a crackling fire. This wasn't the city with its nosey, cacophonous hubbub of people and structure and rules. This was the woods. The antithesis of civilization. There were no rules here and people got lost here every day. And who was to blame when that happened? Not people. The woods. Disappearing out here happens all the time. And every time it does people ask, *How?* not *Who?*

"I want to tell you something before I start slurring my speech," said Louie.

Hart threw an empty can of beer into the fire. "What is it, you inarticulate bastard?"

"Danielle and I are calling it quits. She's taking half my stuff. You want another beer?"

"Wow. Yes."

"Huh?" said Louie.

"Yes, I would like another beer."

"Oh." Louie reached into the cooler and tossed Hart a beer.

"That's a damn shame. I always thought you guys were good together."

Louie exhaled and stared at the fire.

"But hey, that's what these girls do," Hart continued. "They rope you in when you're young, suck the life out of you, take half your stuff and sit back and collect alimony. So what happened?"

"She's cheating on me, Pal. You believe that?"

"Really."

"Really. Let me tell you, Buddy, you don't know how good you have it. Summer would never cheat on you." Louie shook his head. "She's a great girl. You really got it good. So how is Summer?"

"Summer's Summer. She's steady, like a clock."

"That's good."

"Yeah? You ever hear anyone talk about clocks and excitement in the same sentence?"

Louie smiled. "You ever hear anyone talk about drama and peace of mind in the same sentence? You got it good, trust me."

Hart laughed and then shook his head. "Man, I gotta tell you. All these years, I've kind of been envious of you. You got a great job. You make a lot of money."

"Yeah, the job's great. *Was* great. Now I'm giving half my money to her."

They drank in silence, Louie staring at the vastness of the night sky; Hart poking at the fire with a stick, his eyes scanning the forest. *If someone lost his way in the forest and no one was there to hear him— or her—could her death be pinned on anyone? Good question.* Hart felt nervous. He stopped drinking, suddenly feeling afraid that if he got much drunker he might ask the question aloud.

Finally, Louie put his drink down and clapped his hands together once, and smiled with as much enthusiasm as he could muster. "Hey, what can you do? You play the cards you're dealt and you live with it. That's just the way it is."

Brandy lay naked, her toes weaving in and out of Hart's chest hair like a child playing in the grass. "So do you think she suspects anything?"

"Ow!" yelled Hart, as Brandy's pinkie toe clenched when it should have run through.

Laying head to toe behind her, Hart's immediate reaction was to drag his unkempt toenails across Brandy's back, but he made a conscious decision to restrain himself.

"Sorry," said Brandy in a sing-songy way. Hart managed a weak smile as he caressed her leg. "Well?" she asked.

Hart shrugged. "Yeah?"

"I asked if you think she suspects anything."

"Nah. She's clueless."

"Good," said Brandy. "How about your friend Louie? You haven't mentioned anything to him, have you?"

"No, I've been really careful. But hey, guess what? Louie and Danielle are calling it quits. She's taking half his stuff."

"No way."

Hart raised his eyebrows and nodded. "Yep." Again Brandy clutched Hart's chest hair with her toes.

"Ow! Shit, Brandy!"

Brandy laughed. "I'm sorry, Baby. I'm sorry."

"Jeez, my chest isn't a welcome mat. What are you laughing about?"

"I'm sorry," Brandy said through snorts of laughter. "You're just so cute."

"That's true, but why don't we change positions anyway." He started to shift his body.

"No, no, I'll be good."

"Maybe you should wear mittens on your feet," said Hart, his body relaxing again.

"Stop it. I said I'll be careful."

"Fine. Like it's *so* important to remain in this uncomfortable position."

"Anyway." She rolled her eyes, her amusement apparently having vanished. "What happened to Louie isn't going to happen to you. We have to be extra careful. If we're caught, there goes the life insurance."

"Well, let's get this show on the road then. When I was out there fishing, I was thinking, this is it. The woods. It's the perfect place. No one's around. It could be dangerous, and it's hard to find stuff."

Brandy's face twisted a little as she considered it. *The woods.* "Well, first of all, we have to wait a little. I mean you just got the insurance. We don't want any 'accidents' happening too soon. It's too suspicious."

"Okay, so we wait a little. But what do you think about the place?"

"It's perfect. The only problem is, we're talking about Summer. She's afraid of her own shadow. You're never going to get her to go camping, sleeping outside with all those bugs and furry little creatures. She's probably afraid of your chest, for God's sake."

"Or your back."

"Fuck you, Hart."

"Wait a minute. I got it." Hart snapped his fingers and flung his hand open. "Your grandma's cabin. Even Summer would sleep out in the woods if she was indoors."

"You mean Summer's cabin," she corrected and then nodded her head.

"Not for long."

Not bad. She could say one thing about Hart— he was persistent. "You know, Baby, you're not as dumb as you look."

She smiled and then shrieked, "Ow!" as the nail on Hart's big toe dragged across her back.

SIX

IT WAS ANOTHER LAZY Sunday and Hart sat at the kitchen table gnawing on a strip of bacon and reading the morning paper. He was deep in thought and hardly noticed the sniffling that was coming just to his left. He felt stifled, wishing he was somewhere else. What was Brandy doing today? he wondered. *Could I get away with taking another sick day tomorrow?* He was definitely in a rut—hating work all week long, and *thinking* about the upcoming work-week all day Sunday. Something had to change. And soon.

The sniffling got louder, finally forcing Hart to break from his thoughts. He frowned as he looked over at Summer whose shoulders were shaking ever so slightly. "What's wrong?" he asked, hoping he didn't sound quite as annoyed as he felt.

Summer reached out and took Hart's hand. She squeezed it and on instinct, he squeezed back.

Tears coated her eyes, clinging to her lower lids before finally losing their battle with gravity, crashing onto her plate of eggs. "It's been almost six months and I'm still not pregnant."

Hart sighed, in his head, at the thought of this conversation. "Well hey, you said it yourself. It can take a while."

Summer clenched her lips together. "Yeah." She nodded and slowly exhaled. "Yeah. I think I'm going to make an appointment for next week with my ob/ gyn. Maybe she can run some tests and see if anything's wrong."

You mean like the fact that you're on the pill? Hart wondered if that little fact might show up in a test as he looked at her still-full glass of orange juice.

"No, no, wait, wait," Hart said. "Before you do that, I wasn't going to say anything, I wanted it to be a surprise, but I wanted to take you away for a little vacation."

"Really?"

"Yeah, yeah, I think what you need—what *we* need, is just a little R and R. We just need to relax. You know that happened with my friend Chad at work. His wife just couldn't get on the nest. He took her on vacation. Everyone got a little less tense and a month later she was pregnant."

Summer smiled. "Well, that sounds great. Yeah.

Thank you, Hart."

"Absolutely, Honey. My pleasure. Now drink your orange juice. It's good for you."

"You know I think I'll make an appointment with my doctor anyway. I mean why not?" Summer said in between sips.

"Of course, Honey. Absolutely." Hart shrugged.

"But, uh, you know, just wait until we get back. No rush. Let's just relax and then we can take care of business. In the meantime let's not have anything hanging over our heads, you know."

Summer reached over to hug Hart, who reciprocated.

"I love you," she said. "I love you, too."

"So, where are you taking me?"

"Your grandma's cabin."

"I don't know, Hart. It just seems too soon. I mean you just got the life insurance." Brandy replaced her cup of coffee and glared at him.

The restaurant was an out-of-the-way slop joint that was several towns over from where either of them lived. Located in the outskirts of where Hart occasionally made deliveries, he had seen the little eatery many times but had never stopped there before.

"It's been six months," said Hart. "That's not a long time."

"Well what'd you want me to do? She wants to go see her doctor. Her O-P-G-Y-M."

"It's *O-B-G-Y-N*, jackass."

"Yeah, well however you kids are spelling it these days, Summer wants to see him—"

"Her," said Brandy, remembering a brief and uncomfortable encounter with Summer at a medical office a while back.

"Him, her, it, whatever. Will you try to look at the big picture here? If she finds out she's on the pill, she's gonna get suspicious. Then what?"

Brandy ran her fingers through her hair. "What do you see as the big picture, Hart?"

Hart gestured with his hands, a bit annoyed. "Getting the money. Quitting my job and not getting caught."

"Anything else?"

"Uh, living happily ever after? A white picket fence? Clearing up my hemorrhoids? I don't know."

"What about being together?"

Hart's face lost a little color. "Of course. Who do you think the white picket fence is for?"

"Anyway." Brandy twirled her spoon around in her coffee. "Let's get down to the details. If we do a good enough job, this whole insurance thing will be irrelevant. Now I think the woods are great. Like I've said, dumping a body there far off the beaten path is probably almost foolproof. People do get lost in the woods after all. And then the wolves'll help us out and then the snow. And obviously you'll report that she was lost in a whole different area, of course."

Hart's face crinkled as he nodded half-heartedly. "What's the matter?" Brandy asked.

"I don't know. It just seems so, I don't know. It's just lacking somehow. It's too simple."

"Hey simple's good. Don't make it too complicated.

That's how people get caught."

"I don't know. Let's hear the rest of it."

"Well Hart, that's basically it. The only thing left is how are you actually going to, you know—" Brandy looked around. "—do it." She gestured with her eyebrows and tilted her head.

Hart tightened his lips and sat quietly.

A slightly amused, yet annoyed, grin appeared on Brandy's face. "Wait a minute, don't tell me, there's not enough dramatic flair here for you."

"Look, look, it's not just that. What do you want me to do when I'm in the woods? Stab my own wife? Shoot her?"

"It's called *killing*, Hart. What did you have in mind?—tickling her to death?"

"Listen, there's a difference between beating someone to death, you know up close, and uh, cutting a rope that has a piano attached to it, let's say."

Brandy puffed up like a rooster, preparing to let loose.

Hart put his hands up. "It's just an analogy. I'm just saying."

Brandy exhaled, rubbing her thumb and forefinger along the bridge of her nose. "Hart, let's just keep it simple. Poison her if you don't want to get your hands dirty."

"That's been done to death." Hart laughed, realizing what he just said. "Besides that kills the whole woods idea, and I don't know how to score poison."

"Why don't we just tie her to a train, Snidely Whiplash? You're not one of James Bond's nemeses. Just keep it simple, Hart. No suspenseful hourglasses and contraptions and gizmos and dramatic flair. We're not trying to create an exciting cliffhanger. We just want this to work."

"Look, I'm the one actually doing this. Don't worry, okay? I'll come up with something. Why don't you draw up a map of the area and your grandma's property for me."

Hart turned over a paper placemat for her sketch. "Look, don't worry," he continued. "Creative doesn't have to mean complicated."

SEVEN

S O GO SOMEWHERE else if you don't like the cabin." Bob looked especially good today. Maybe it was the fact that the firm's latest partner and eternal heartthrob had recently won a particularly impressive case. It seemed to make him all that much more attractive to every female in the firm—if that was possible. As the only one in the office who really had any kind of meaningful shot at Bob, his increasing appeal was not lost on Summer, despite her preoccupations.

She watched his mouth as his words glided effortlessly off of his tongue. He had an air of immense confidence that he seemed to exude brilliantly without the slightest hint of arrogance. And it all came so naturally, faltering only slightly in the presence of Summer, who either didn't notice or didn't care—about the faltering, that is.

As Bob strode toward her, Summer smiled, as did all of the other women in the office, secretly hoping he'd stop at her desk.

Summer loved when he approached her, even though it was usually to simply ask for files or to retrieve messages. But it was the small talk in between that she really adored. The jokes, the harmless flirting. But that was all it was. She knew it could never be any more than that. She loved Hart and wasn't the type of person to be caught up in such girlish fantasies. At least not in real life. No, Bob was great but she could tell the difference between love and infatuation.

"No," she said. "I think I'll stick to the cabin. Hart's really excited about it and I don't want to disappoint him. Besides, I technically own it—the cabin, I mean—so the vacation wouldn't really cost much and we really need to save our money right now." She shrugged. "We're trying for a baby."

Bob raised his eyebrows and nodded, smiling weakly. "Oh. How long have you been trying for?" Then he reddened a little and cringed. "Wow. That was really personal." Then he feigned an uppercut to his own chin, making a loud clicking sound-effect with his tongue in the process. "Please don't answer that. I shouldn't have asked and the only way I can redeem myself now is if you ignore me."

Summer laughed. "It's okay, Bob."

"Hey, it's the only way I'll learn," said Bob, now smiling, his confidence returning.

"It's fine. And to answer your question, it's been about six months."

"Ahh, I told you not to tell me," said Bob, playfully waving his hand in the air.

"Am I fired?"

"No, no, I'm the one who's fired. I'm fired up about you having a baby. That's great news."

"Thanks. We'll see what happens. Six months seems like a long time to me, but I guess when it's right, it's right."

If there's anything I can do to help, just let me know, immediately jumped into Bob's head but instead he said, "Absolutely."

Bob smiled and she smiled back. He had so much work to do but didn't want the conversation to end.

"So what's the deal with this cabin?" he asked. "Is it haunted or something?"

"I was just never that crazy about it. My cousin Brandy always loved it and my grandma should have probably left it to her to tell you the truth. I guessed she felt sorry for me because I had just lost my parents. Honestly, I haven't been there in twenty years. It just kind of gives me the creeps. My Uncle Frank died there."

Bob cocked his head, curious.

"It was kind of weird. A tree limb just spontaneously dropped. I think it was an oak. It hit him in the head and he died. Anyway, it's not that. I'm just not that crazy about the woods. You know, wild animals and all that."

Bob smiled at her. God she was cute. "I guess I'm just being silly, huh?"

Bob shook his head. "I think you're the bravest woman that ever lived."

Summer laughed. "You're crazy."

He smiled again and patted her hand. And then she screamed.

Bob pulled his hand back, looking stunned. "What?"

Summer put both hands over her mouth, stifling her own outburst. Then she pointed to the corner of her desk and whispered, "A spider."

Bob grinned, shaking his head. "Do yourself a favor and pick a new vacation spot."

EIGHT

I GOT THE PERFECT SPOT." Hart was unsuccessfully suppressing a smile. He figured Brandy wouldn't be too wild about it but didn't particularly care. It was his idea. He was taking all the risks. He would be the one actually doing it. Besides, he decided, doing something as big as this did require some dramatic flair, and he wasn't going to apologize for it either. Being mundane went against who he was.

Even in school when a teacher would go around the room and have everyone introduce himself, Hart couldn't stand the idea of simply stating his name and who his last English teacher was. He had to come up with something funny. Something memorable, creative. Not just be like everybody else.

Brandy finished her sip of Coke and put the can back down on her kitchen table. She felt skeptical, but anxious to hear what Hart had come up with.

"You mean you don't want to do it in the woods anymore?" she said.

"I mean the perfect spot *in* the woods," he answered.

Brandy put her elbow on the table, faced her open hand straight up and glided her chin into her waiting palm. "Well I hope your plan doesn't require you to twirl your mustache between your fingers as the audience hisses and pelts you with tomatoes."

"No audience, wise guy. So, I was looking at this map of Granny's property that you drew up for me." He pulled the map out of his front pocket and unfolded it. "It's a nice spread. How many acres did you say it was?"

"A few hundred."

Hart nodded. "Good. Now what really caught my eye was this." Hart pointed to the map as Brandy leaned in. "This footbridge. How long is it?"

"I don't know."

"Would you say it's like the distance between first and second base on a baseball field?"

Brandy started to feel impatient but forced herself to relax. This was Hart we were talking about and this whole thing was going to unfold in his own way in his own time. Experience had taught her that. "I guess about that. What, a hundred feet?"

"And how far down? Below the bridge, I mean."

"Five hundred, sixty-three feet," she said.

"Are you serious? Five hundred, sixty-three feet?

You know it exactly?"

"Yeah, I do. My Uncle Frank measured it when I was a kid. It was a big deal in our family. He climbed down the gorge, camped for a night and climbed back up the next day."

"It only took a day to climb back up?"

Brandy nodded. "I don't remember. Maybe eight hours or so. Something like that. The north side of the gorge, according to Uncle Frank, basically has almost like, um, stairs kind of. Like natural stairs. There were only a few spots, he said, that were a little tough, that required some rope, but yeah, it's pretty cool. He actually wanted to take Summer and me down and back up. Of course Summer was scared to death and didn't want to do it. I did at the time, but after Uncle Frank fell off that bridge, to his death, I pretty much lost interest, too."

"Wait a minute. He fell off the bridge? Summer told me a tree fell on him or something. A big branch from an oak tree or something."

"Yeah well, that's what they told her when she was a kid so she wouldn't be so freaked out."

"Well, that was stupid. There are a lot more trees in the world than bridges. Weren't they worried that she'd be afraid of trees after that?"

Brandy began tapping the table with her fingers now. "I don't know, Hart. She's afraid of everything. What's the difference? You gonna tell me about your plan already?"

"Okay, listen. When me and Summer are up there, I'm going to suggest we take a walk. When we get to the bridge, I'm going to go first. It's a narrow bridge, right? Halfway across I'll tell her that I forgot something on the other side and I need her to go back and get it for me. It's a narrow bridge, so she's not going to want me to go around her—she'll be too freaked out—so she'll turn around and go get it for me—"

"Wait a minute, Agatha Christie. Hold on. You're right, she's going to be freaked out. What makes you think she'll even go across the bridge in the first place?"

"I'll tell you in a second. Hold on, let me finish."

Brandy looked to the side and tossed her hands in the air.

"Anyway, where the hell was I? So I'll pre-plant my gloves or something in the bushes for Summer to go back to get. In the meantime, I'll cross over to the other side of the bridge and when Summer's got my gloves and she's halfway across, snip-snip, I cut the ropes on the bridge. No matter which side she runs to as I'm cutting, she'll never make it."

Brandy started to talk but Hart continued, throwing his hand up, traffic cop style. "I know what you're going to say. How can I cut the rope so fast? Heavy, heavy duty bolt cutters made for cable. It'll be fast. And they'll be pre-planted on the other side of the gorge so I can grab them quick. Brandy, it's going to work."

"Hart, why do you have to make it so complicated? Just *push* her off the gorge. And if you say dramatic flair one more time I'm going to stick my foot up your ass."

"Hey, I'm not going to mine for gold with a thousand swings of my pick when I can just blow the fuckin' thing up with one push of a button." He had that little beauty planned out and ready to go.

Brandy sighed as the palm of her hand rolled off her chin and onto forehead. After a moment, she straightened up. "I guess I shouldn't be surprised. Okay, I guess it'll work. It just seems like way too much effort to me, but what do I know? So fill me in. Then what? After her fall?"

Hart smiled. "I wait a few days and tell the cops that Summer took a walk in the woods while I did some errands in town. Make sure people see me. Tell the cops that she was hiking over here." Hart pointed to a part of the map off of Grandma's property and far from the gorge. "I'm sure people get lost in the woods every day. With no police record and no body…" Hart smiled and raised his hands in the air as if to say, *What can the cops do?* "And if they do find the body, well, I guess she fell down. What links that to me?"

Brandy started to talk, but Hart was on a roll and stopped her. "Okay, so what about the cops and the bridge? Why is the bridge cut? I got it all figured out. Before we walk across the bridge, a day or two before, I go to work. I'll go to the other side of the bridge, untie it and put some slack in it and re-tie it. That way, when I cut it, I'll still have some rope to re-tie it later, after the princess' fall from grace. Or instead of cutting the rope, maybe I'll just put a few slipknots in the rope and untie it when Summer's on the bridge. Either way. I'll bring the bolt cutters just in case. I thought about just removing the bridge after Summer's gone, but there are probably satellite pictures somewhere of the property. Besides, that's a pretty big bridge to try to get rid of. So, what do you think?"

"How are you going to get back across the bridge after it's cut?" she asked.

Brandy watched as the smile dissolved from Hart's face. She really preferred the simple approach, but took no joy in his enthusiasm being stymied. "And don't say the gorge's 'stairs.' Those are only on the north side—the side you'd be on when you cut the rope, so that's not going to help you, unless you want to go down the gorge and back up on the same side just for the—"

"I get it. I get it. Alright, alright, this is why it's good to talk about it. I'm actually a little pissed at you right now, but I'm glad you're bringing it up."

Brandy smiled. "I know what to do."

"What?"

"When you're sabotaging things on the other side of the bridge, you attach a long rope to the bridge. Just make sure it's longer than the width of the gorge. After she falls, you just pull the bridge up with the rope and re-tie the bridge."

Hart's smile was back as he gently shook his head. "That's great. I love you Baby."

"I love you, too, Hart." She said it like she must be some kind of idiot.

They stood up and hugged each other.

"Oh, and to make sure you don't lose that long piece of rope, tie the other end to a tree. And lay it on the ground and cover it with dirt so it can't be seen," she continued.

"Excellent." *Now* you *have dramatic flair,* he thought. But he wasn't going to say it.

Then she suddenly broke their embrace. "Wait a minute. Before we break out the champagne, you never told me how you plan on getting her on that bridge in the first place. Summer's afraid of her own shadow. And that bridge scares the hell out of her."

"Relax. I'll guilt her into it. I got her to take flying lessons for God's sake. This'll be a piece of cake."

Brandy exhaled loudly. "Wouldn't it just be easier to push her?"

No dramatic flair whatsoever, he thought. But he wasn't going to say it.

NINE

SUMMER CAREFULLY ARRANGED the pens and pencils in the top drawer of her desk at work. There was nothing she hated more than not knowing where things were. It drove her crazy that Hart was the exact opposite but was so sweet about it that she rarely talked to him about his messiness, preferring to quietly straighten things herself. If she did mention anything to him, it was always done with a certain gentle grace that left Hart feeling good about himself. A little too good, as he never felt the need to accommodate Summer in the least.

Summer's fetish for order was, in a sense, paradoxically offset by a certain clumsiness that often threatened the structure she craved. She was her own worst enemy in this regard—building the perfect sandcastle, everything just so, but inevitably being the one to lay it flat far in advance of anyone else or Mother Nature herself.

Picking up a pencil, she swiveled her chair toward her personal calendar which was standing up on the left side of her desk. Moving a bit too fast, the tip of her pencil struck the calendar, breaking the cone-shaped lead off in the process. Without pause, her eyes hunted for the wayward piece, which she quickly spied and disposed of. Then she swiveled her chair in the other direction and resharpened her pencil, an act followed without hesitation by the cleansing of her lead-stained hand with a "wipey." Ever since she was a little girl and in every class she ever took, she always insisted upon having a least three sharp pencils at the ready. And of course, work would be no different.

Back to the calendar, two events stood out for her: her trip to the woods with Hart and her appointment with her ob/gyn. The appointment was three weeks away. Despite her talk with Hart, she had decided to make her appointment anyway. After all, she could get her R and R and still be ready to discuss things with Dr. Stillwell, pregnant or still trying. Either way, she'd want to consult with her doctor, and knowing that she had an appointment was one less thing to think about and helped to put her further at ease. Besides, her periods had been far more regular than they had ever been when she had been off the pill in the past. Something she had been wondering about for a few months now.

Hart wasn't too happy about the appointment at first, but realized right away that if he ranted too much, it would seem suspicious. "Whatever works for you, Honey," he had commented, careful to come off in a gentle, unalarmed way. He had planned to tell Brandy about it, but then it hit him that the appointment was a good thing. It only strengthened his case for why they had needed life insurance: they wanted children and the appointment, which was set weeks after Summer's unfortunate demise, would only serve to make his case. This realization put Hart at ease and he forgot all about sharing the news with Brandy.

The other big event, her trip to the woods with Hart, was set for the coming weekend. Despite her apprehensions, and the obvious predominance of the number of spiders in the woods compared to that in the city, she was growing more and more excited. The trip would be for a full week and she was determined to try new things, relax and truly enjoy herself. Besides spending more time with Hart than she had in a long time, Summer was also excited about getting more flying time in. With an airfield just an hour north of her grandma's cabin, Hart happily agreed that she should have a day to herself to pursue her newfound hobby. Summer was thrilled that Hart was so accommodating as she had been dying to get more flying hours, each of which contributed toward her pilot's license. Between work, karate, school and general social engagements, the hours had been hard to come by of late. This vacation had so many nice elements to it and Summer couldn't help but feel grateful for it all.

The hand on her shoulder was warm and gentle, but she nevertheless jumped and let out a gasp which bordered on a stifled scream. She also flipped her pencil in the air and watched it, in what seemed like slow motion, crash down on her desk, the tip breaking once again. The hand, it turned out, belonged to Bob, office heartthrob.

"Oh, sorry if I scared you," he said, unable to stop a chuckle which was filled far more with adoration than any trace of ridicule. He delighted in these "Summer moments", as he called them.

"I just sharpened that, too," she said sheepishly, glancing up at Bob. Then without delay, she wiped her hands and re-sharpened her battle-worn pencil.

"Don't worry about it. As a partner here, I can get you as many pencils as you want." He smiled.

She smiled back. "Well I guess it pays to know people in high places." She crossed her legs.

Bob felt his face get hot. "Yeah, uh, well especially with the huge pencil shortage going on these days."

"It's terrible, isn't it?" she said, shaking her head. "Ahh, I could tell you stories." He nodded and smiled again. "So, you all ready for the big vacation?"

"What?" she said. "Oh, yeah, yeah, the vacation, absolutely."

"Good, good."

They were silent and Bob buried his hands in his pockets. He kicked at some imaginary dirt at the immaculately-kept carpeting.

"Was there something I can get you, Mr. Day?"

"No. No. Oh, and please call me Bob."

"Really? It would be so much easier to call you Mr. Day," she said, her head dropping a little like a puppy dog. "I call all the other partners Mister. They seem to expect it."

"Well, I hope I'm not like all the other partners."

"No, you're not." She held her gaze.

"Listen, I shouldn't bother you with this, but…"

"I'm sure it's fine. What is it?"

"Well I was just thinking I should get your cell phone number just in case I can't find something here at work. I mean, you're so organized. But forget it. I don't want to bother you on vacation. Forget I brought it up."

"It's alright, Bob. It's no big deal." *I'm sure my number's in my files*, she thought, but really didn't mind giving it to him. Besides, she felt he might be embarrassed if she mentioned the files. So she jotted her number down and handed it to him.

"Thanks." He took out a business card from his jacket pocket. "Let me just jot down my cell number."

"Sure," she said, but they were both wondering the same thing. Why—or what was the pretense for why— would she need his cell phone number?

He handed her the card. "Here you go. Hey you never know. Let's say you're about to eat some ivy up there and you want to know if it's poisonous or not, give me a call. I was an eagle scout."

A few forced jokes later, about ivy being off her menu since the third grade and how forests were teeming with legal briefs these days, and Bob was walking back to his office. His head was held high, but his chin felt like it was dragging on the ground as he rolled his eyes and cursed himself.

She, on the other hand, was smiling. *Adorable. If I wasn't so happily married…*

TEN

HART PACKED HIS BAG like a cartoon character might. One quickly-built giant pile of clothes on the bed was just as quickly bear-hugged and deposited into his only suitcase. Heavily scuffed, his imitation leather-gilded bag had been through the wringer. After stuffing anything back in that happened to be sticking out, he closed the suitcase and fastened the latch. Then he grabbed it, as well as one good-sized semi-filled backpack, and loaded them into his Acura TSX. Summer's Santa Fe would have made a lot more sense but Hart hated that car and didn't think it was reliable, even though it had never given Summer a bit of trouble.

"Are you ready?" he bellowed as he re-entered the house, knowing damn well she wasn't.

"Almost." Unlike Hart, Summer was very meticulous about her packing. Anything that could potentially spill or leak, like hand cream or shampoo, was deposited individually in a plastic bag before being laid in her suitcase. Her shoes were turned sole to sole and also placed in a plastic bag so they would not touch her clean clothes. And unlike her husband, she rarely forgot anything when packing.

Interstate 5 seemed to be wide open. A real relief to Hart who was so sick and tired of driving everyday on his job that he could just scream—and often did.

"You okay with the Eagles?" he asked, tuning around the dial and pausing at the song, "Take it Easy."

"Sure," Summer said. She smiled to herself. She didn't know if it was her impending pregnancy or what, but Hart had been so nice to her lately that she beamed inside. She loved the little touches. The hand-holding. Asking her if she was okay with his music in the car. Things that he had neglected to do for years.

"Thanks again, Hart, for not minding about me taking a day to go flying. I know we're trying to spend time together."

"No problem. This is your vacation, too. I want it to be memorable." He smiled at her and she took his hand. *Besides, while you're away flying, I'll have time to sabotage the bridge.* He squeezed her hand.

It also flashed in his mind that she might die while flying. It was pretty remote but there was always the chance. It would sure make things easier, but it might not be such a good thing. He'd probably have to prove to the insurance company that she had taken up flying lesson *after* she had taken out her policy. Easy enough to do, but they might not like it and could put up a fight. All in all, it would be best if he handled her passing, himself.

Besides, there was something about executing his own plan that gave him some perverse delight. Like he was hatching some brilliant jewel heist. There was some strange satisfaction to it all like it somehow deemed him a self-made man versus someone who wins the lottery through pure luck.

Summer looked out the window. She felt so happy. So free. Any anxiety she felt about the woods seemed to float to the back burner. This was her time. Hart had been right. She really did need some R and R. She thought about the words. Rest and Relaxation. They sounded so nice. *For one week, I'm not going to worry about anything. Not spiders, the dark woods, wild animals, tidying up the cabin, getting pregnant, nothing. Total R and R.*

She pressed the side of her face against the passenger side window, the green sign ahead inching closer. She smiled.

Cardsdale 280 miles.

———————————

Brandy Hastling felt good. This was to be her first summer vacation in three years. And if things went well, she'd eventually be quitting her job as assistant manager at The Pet Expo very soon now. She thoroughly disliked the job and it was one that, in her words, she was "very much over-qualified for." It was only too bad that she had let so much vacation time build up, because now, with her impending wealth just a few days away, it looked as if she'd never get a chance to use it.

She would be staying one hour south of Cardsdale at a little out-of-the-way motel called the Blue Jay Inn. The accommodations, as she was well aware, would not be nearly as lovely and whimsical as its name suggested. But she didn't much care. Good times were just around the corner.

Initially she wasn't too thrilled with the idea of being so close to the location of Summer's murder, but Hart had insisted.

"I'm the one taking all the risks here," he had said. "And if anything goes wrong, I'm going to need you near me." She would be an hour away. Close enough to get to Hart quickly if he called her, but far enough away that nobody would be bumping into anyone accidentally.

Brandy had stayed at the Blue Jay a few times before and it gave her some comfort that this "Mom and Pop" motel out in the middle of nowhere could at least serve as some type of alibi for her whereabouts if push came to shove.

But as things often go, events would not work out as planned.

It was two days into Summer and Hart's trip when Brandy set off on her own vacation. She had worked a long day and was exhausted. As she drove up I-5, her mind was going a mile a minute. Mentally, she felt good, excited. But she was also in a bit of a frenzy as thoughts and ideas poured in. This was really happening. She and Hart would soon be free of their burdensome jobs and money troubles forever. And they would be together, just the two of them. No more sneaking around.

She finally had to stop herself as her head felt like it would explode if she attempted to think of so much at once. Instead, she tried to concentrate on her driving and on her off-ramp—Bort Road.

The miles passed beneath her tires in the most indistinct way. Her eyelids were getting heavy now and she was forced to slap herself a few times to stay awake. If only she could get some goddamn coffee, but she knew that was useless. There was simply nothing around. "Bort Road, Bort Road," her lips chanted breathlessly. "B-o- r-t, Bort Road," she said as she read the white letters on the small green sign blurring by. Shit! She had passed it. "Dammit!" she screamed. Her eyes widened as a shot of adrenaline filled her head. She clutched the steering wheel, willing it to turn around. Taking a deep breath, she strained to see the sign up ahead: *Cornhinter Way 12 miles* it read.

Maybe she could just back up on the freeway, she thought, an idea complicated by a pair of headlights that went zooming by. As the car passed, it launched a long drawn out honk clearly meant for her. She had slowed down quite a bit and now realized that yet another car was bearing down on her. So she pressed the gas hard and watched in her rearview mirror as the car swerved around her, this one thankfully laying off the horn. It didn't look like backing up was going to be an option.

The next eleven and a half miles were a virtual cacophony of yelling, slapping and singing with heavy doses of blasting music and the faint sound of Brandy's head intermittently banging backwards against the headrest. Anything to stay awake.

She toyed with the thought of pulling over to the shoulder of the freeway, but the idea of being struck by some drunken asshole while she slept, dissuaded her.

She could make it, she told herself. God, she was tired. If she missed the Cornhinter off ramp, she'd have to kill herself, she muttered as she stuck hard to the far right lane.

"Yes!" she whooped, as she turned her wheel to the right, exiting the freeway at last. Pure darkness. No hotels, no coffee shop, no nothing. Just sleep.

She drove about thirty feet before she pulled off the road, next to some large overgrown bushes. Killing the engine, she couldn't pull the seat lever fast enough, dead to the world before she was fully reclined. The Blue Jay Inn could go to hell.

ELEVEN

HUNCKE'S SERVICE STATION had stopped serving deli food a long time ago. And while some businesses that have been around for decades manage to maintain a certain charm wrapped in its glory of yesteryear, Huncke's personified none of this. Its worn out rusticity was the living embodiment of a functional and aloof shell where weary travelers and indifferent locals got gas and pre-packaged snacks—not necessarily in that order.

Grandma had remembered Mrs. Huncke's fresh homemade apple pie and Summer had vague recollections of Huncke's soft-serve ice cream. But those days were long gone and as Hart pulled his car into the station, Summer arched her back and stretched, seeing no reason to exit the car to visit this outdated relic "for old time's sake" or any other reason.

"Dammit," Hart yelled as he cut the engine. "What is it?" asked Summer, her heavy eyelids springing open.

Hart pointed out the driver's side window at a crudely written sign: *NO GAS TODAY sorry*

"It's okay, Honey," Summer said. "We'll get gas tomorrow. We have enough to drive around town for a little while until then."

"I guess," Hart said. *Stupid hick little town. This kind of thing never happens in the city.* He reached for the key.

"Wait," she said. "Let's take a break. You've been driving for a long time. Why don't you get yourself a snack inside? Oh, and some breakfast stuff for tomorrow."

Hart shrugged. "Alright. You coming?"

Summer yawned and stretched again. "No thanks, I'm fine."

When Hart exited the car, his nostrils filled with the fragrant and familiar scent of pine. It was a whole different world out here, he thought. He couldn't help but notice a certain freshness that permeated the air, and the wonderful background soundtrack that just a few scattered birds were providing.

And then the city was back. Beelining straight toward him was a hippie drifter, his hand out. "Brother, can you spare a dime?" may have been the appropriate opener had Huncke's maintained its original 1930's constitution. The drifter's eyes were dead but penetrating. His entire hue, almost a dull sepia, as if he was fairly rusting away. He was the personification of a living, breathing monochromatic being, brought about by a complete covering of the same dust from head to toe.

A cigarette dangling loosely from his lips, the man was clearly on something, and he approached in a manner that was difficult to ignore. But Hart was ready. Unlike most people, he didn't mind confronting the homeless. He almost relished it and often screwed around with them for his own amusement. If anything, Hart was more irritated by the shattering of his bucolic surroundings that he rarely got to experience in his everyday life.

Nevertheless, the situation was what it was and Hart decided to use one of his favorites from his transient "bag of tricks". He watched the man carefully and just as the man was about to open his mouth, Hart quickly injected, "Hey can you spare a dollar?"

"Huh?" was the homeless man's only response, as if he had suddenly found himself on stage with a seasoned ad-libber during what should have otherwise been a well-rehearsed play. He stopped dead in his tracks and crinkled his forehead.

Hart smirked to himself. Works every time.

Summer watched from the car. And cringed. She had seen Hart do this kind of thing many times before and it always made her nervous and uncomfortable, fearing for both the homeless person's feelings and Hart's safety. She didn't have to wait long, however, to see how this one would play out.

"Get the hell out of here!" yelled Whitman, the owner of Huncke's, as he sprayed a hose on the homeless man. Positioned as if he was holding a bayonet, he looked ready for a fight.

With water streaking down his face, the homeless man shook his head, his clothing and skin seeming to turn a shade or two lighter.

"And put that cigarette out, you dumbshit. This is a gas station," continued Whitman, concentrating the blast of water at the man's mouth.

As the doused cigarette flew from his lips, the man took a few steps toward Whitman, opening his mouth long enough to bark like a dog. Then he stopped walking and added, "Fuck you, Huncke! I'll be back. And thanks for shower, old man. I needed one anyway."

"You sure do, you degenerate!" retorted Whitman. The homeless man turned on his heels. Walking away he flipped the bird with both hands, an evil cackling coloring the scene.

Shutting the hose off, Whitman turned to Hart. "Sorry about all that."

Hart shrugged. "No problem. I'm just thrilled to get away from the hubbub of the city and out to the tranquility of the woods once in a while."

Whitman laughed. "Yeah well, welcome to Cardsdale."

———————————————

Five minutes after loading up the car with snacks and groceries, and some jawing with Whitman, Hart and Summer were on their way. Over the river and through the woods to Grandmother's house they went, the roads narrow and windy but relatively flat at this point, the scene picturesque, calm and inviting. "I forgot how beautiful it was up here," Summer said.

"So are you, Honey."

Summer's eyes lit up. "Thank you, Hart."

He put his arm around and her and she snuggled into his body.

She smiled. "I'm so glad you thought of this. You picked the perfect spot."

Summer's eyes lit up. "Thank you, Hart."

He put his arm around her and she snuggled into his body.

She smiled. "I'm so glad you thought of this. You picked the perfect spot."

"I think so."

Grandma's house was located on Snug Lodge Way and was one of only three houses on a road that didn't even have a name until 1942—or possibly 1943; the records were unclear on the matter. And it was Summer and Brandy's grandmother herself who named the road, being that she was the longest living resident in the vicinity.

Each house on Snug Lodge Way sat on numerous acres of land, and all three served as summer retreats for their primarily absent owners.

And much like Snug Lodge itself—the name of Grandma's house—the other two homes had been in their respective family for several generations. The isolation was quaint by some standards and lonesome by others, but it was, if nothing else, palpable.

Snug Lodge's name was well deserved. Less than a thousand square feet, it was comfortable with a fairly open floor plan, but a design nonetheless that left most guests with a desire to explore the great outdoors.

The house was set back a good quarter mile from the "main road," and the grounds were ninety-nine percent the work of Mother Nature herself. Dense clusters of pine trees dominated, but there was no shortage of beautiful wildflowers, paths and boulders and rocks of varying sizes, whose glittery speckles popped against their variegated backdrop.

But the highlight of the property was, of course, the magnificent gorge that sat about a mile or so from the back of Grandma's house. Its beauty lay in the variety it lent to the natural setting at large and in the skill with which it seemed to be harmoniously carved from the earth; its natural "stairs" serving as an irresistible siren between an untamed wilderness and man's unquenchable desire to ingratiate himself. To tame the untamable.

Hart stopped the car. He was unimpressed. All he saw was a shack. A piece of crap that could only remain in a family for sentimental reasons. As soon as Summer's body was cold enough to ever link him to any wrongdoings, he'd push Brandy to sell this place.

Summer's eyes were glazed over. She stared at the cabin. When she finally did blink, she felt the meandering wetness of her tears as they ambled down her cheeks. The tears, as well as the lump in her throat, surprised the hell out of her. Thoughts of her grandmother, her poor dead uncle Frank and a host of other memories gushed into her brain without warning.

Both out of the car now, Hart looked over at her. "You okay?" he asked.

"Yeah. Yeah, I'm fine."

"About like you remember it?"

"Yeah. More or less."

Oh, it's gotta be less, he thought, suppressing the urge to say it out loud. He walked to the back of the car and she followed suit. He popped the trunk and looked over at Summer.

"You sure you're okay?" he said. Summer smiled. "I'm fine. Thanks."

"Come here." He embraced her.

She squeezed him back.

"Don't cry, Honey. We don't have to stay long." She laughed.

"Besides," he continued. "I hear they're under new management."

They broke their embrace and she hit him playfully. "You're terrible. It's not that bad."

"Hey, you're the one crying. Here. Why don't you go ahead. I'll get the stuff." He handed her the keys to the house.

"Are you sure you don't want any help?" she asked. Hart looked down at a bag inside the trunk that he didn't recognize. He could have sworn he had put his bolt cutters and some rope in that area. He felt his heart start to rev up.

"What's this?" he asked, trying not to sound panicked. He pointed at the unfamiliar bag.

"Just my stuff for flying." She picked up the bag. "Oh. Oh."

"Something wrong?" she asked.

"What? No. No. I just didn't recognize it at first.

Listen, go ahead. I'll get everything else."

The cabin was outdated but Summer quickly made up her mind that she liked it, and appreciated it. As she walked around, more memories flooded back. Any apprehensions she may have had about the woods seemed to melt away.

Hart had taken several trips to get everything in and was now unloading things in the main bedroom.

"Dammit," he yelled. "What is it?"

"I don't believe this. My deodorant and toothpaste ran all over my clothes. And shit! I forgot my brush. And my underwear."

Summer laughed to herself so he couldn't hear her.

"It's okay, you can borrow a pair of mine."

"Thanks."

Same old Hart. She had warned him that the altitude might make everything leak out and that bottles and tubes should be bagged…

Summer strained her ears for a moment. Hart's ranting and raving seemed to have stopped. She looked at the lace curtains in the kitchen and thought of Grandma. Maybe Wolfe was wrong. Maybe you can go home again.

TWELVE

THE REST OF THE DAY proved to be relaxing, at least for Summer. Hart managed to remain pretty cool on the outside, but his insides were an assemblage of calculations. Technically he was on vacation, but mentally he had never worked harder. He was constantly on the scout. Walks in the woods were reconnaissance missions. Monuments to beauty became hiding spots, traps, weapons.

Solid, uninterrupted thinking was impossible for Hart. He was either talking, to seem engaged, or listening to what Summer had to say.

"Hart? Hart? Did you hear what I just said?"

"Huh," he replied, lost for a moment in thought.

"I'm sorry, Honey. Say it one more time, please."

He couldn't let that happen too often. She'd wonder what was going on. Or, worse, it might result in an argument. That could kill his whole plan. He needed her unwitting cooperation. Maybe she'd go flying soon and he'd have the whole place to himself. *Yeah, that's what I'll do. Just relax. No need to sneak around. I'll have plenty of time when she goes off flying.*

One thing nagging at him, for some reason, was his near-empty gas tank. Maybe it was from years of driving for a living. What if he needed to beat it out of there for some reason? Not having much gas somehow made him feel vulnerable. He knew, of course, he'd take care of it, but for now it was just one more thing to think about.

Hart and Summer held hands as they walked. Sometimes he'd put his arm around her and she'd snuggle in close to him, their legs almost moving in unison to a pleasant and gentle beat. They were on forest time and the tranquility of it all seemed to envelope them both. Their talking was soft and harmonious, almost hypnotically weaving into the natural background of the forest—the birds and other wildlife, the ever-present white noise that's so smooth and soothing and always there if you just let it be.

And suddenly it appeared. The gorge. It was raw and beautiful, and would be Summer's final resting place. Hart moved toward it, holding Summer's hand. It was different than he had pictured it, not in a negative way, but just because that's how life always is. The contrast between conception and reality was evident and Hart was eager to get a better look.

At a certain distance from the edge of the gorge, Summer began to feel a little a stiff. The closer they got, the stiffer she became. Finally she stopped.

"What's the matter, Honey?" he asked. "Nothing. This is just as close as I want to get, that's all."

"Really? We're not that close," he said. *Shit, is this going to be a problem now?* Hart looked around. It was so quiet, so isolated. A feeling came over him like he and Summer were the last two people on earth. He let his imagination take over for a moment. What if they *were* the last two people on earth? No one's around. What if I killed her right now? Just dragged her to the edge of the gorge and gave her big shove? Then he laughed to himself. If no else existed, how would I collect my insurance money?

"You okay, Hart?" she asked. "What? Oh yeah."

"Sorry, Hart. I could probably force myself to walk across the bridge, but the edge still makes me nervous."

"Where's the bridge?"

The old hanging bridge was weathered but still looked solid. Simple in construction, its length was a good hundred feet across. The top two ropes, which flanked the bridge on each side, ran horizontally, serving as "handrails" and they were about ¾ inch in diameter. The bottom two ropes, one on each side, served as the primary support of the bridge's deck, and also lay horizontally. Those were a little thicker than the handrails and they too, ran the length of bridge. Between the handrail and the bottom rope, on either side, ran vertical ropes spaced about six to eight inches apart.

The bottom of the bridge, the deck, was made of individual wooden pieces constructed of one by sixes and rectangular in shape. Each end of the bridge, the anchor, was attached to what appeared to be partially sunken railroad ties connected by metal stakes that were driven deep into the earth.

As they looked at the bridge, thoughts of her Uncle Frank crowded Summer's head. Not because he had died there. She hadn't known that. She thought of him because he had always been her tangible reminder that we are all mortal. That things do happen.

The bridge looked pretty much like she had remembered. She hated like hell that she was the only one in the family that was scared of it. There was nothing to be afraid of. Not really. At least that's what she told herself. It was part of growing up. Facing your fears. Conquering them. Besides, she had already chickened out about getting too close to the edge of the gorge. She couldn't let her nerves do her thinking for her.

Hart was already on the bridge as Summer took a deep breath.

"You'll be fine, Honey," he said, putting his hand out for her.

She thought about what a lucky woman she was.

Hart was so sweet. So encouraging.

Exhaling, she stepped on the bridge and held the handrail. Then she nervously screamed and started laughing as she stepped back off.

Hart smiled at her. It was even genuine. *She really is kind of cute.* But on the inside, every organ in his body clenched.

"Okay, okay, okay," she said smiling as she shook her hands. "You can do this."

"Of course you can," said Hart, holding out his hand.

"It's okay, thanks, I'll do it," she said, reaching

instead for the handrail of the bridge. A look of determination came over her face. Left, right, left right. Her hands and feet were working together. She was doing it. She was doing it. A smile appeared on her face. "Good job, Honey," Hart said, walking a few feet ahead of her, occasionally looking back.

She let out a little giggle. "Thanks, Sweetheart. It's beautiful up here."

"It's gorgeous," he said looking down, and suddenly he stopped.

"What's a matter?" she asked.

He turned to face her. "Nothing. I just wanted to absorb it all."

They put their arms around each other and took in the majesty of a great big world. It was beautiful and in some ways Summer never felt safer.

THIRTEEN

AS HE PUT HIS HAND on the back of her neck, Hart couldn't help himself. It was uncontrollable. The thoughts just filled his head of their own volition. And he could see her falling in his mind's eye. Do it now, he thought, and it's all over. No more thinking about it. No more planning. To hell with dramatic flair.

He looked at the handrail. It was about waist high. He couldn't just push her. He'd have to lift her with both hands. And what would her hands be doing? Grabbing, clutching, scratching, clawing. He could do it. Of course he could, but it wouldn't be pretty.

———

As they walked back, Hart and Summer continued holding hands, both satisfied in their own way. Hart because he had come to realize that he liked his original plan. Why violently roll all over a campfire when you can simply stand ten feet away and throw a bucket of water on it? Both ways put out the fire.

He was also pleased that he had now seen everything for himself. The gorge, the bridge, the brush where he'd be hiding his cable cutters. He no longer had to visualize the layout.

And Summer, too, had a little extra spring in her step. She had made it across the bridge. She had done it. Another fear conquered. Well, maybe not conquered, but confronted. If she was to be honest with herself, she had to admit that the bridge still scared the hell out of her, but that's what made what she did today all that much more impressive. She felt proud of herself. She also felt exhausted.

Hart, on the other hand, was bursting with excitement. He couldn't wait to get back to the cabin and take his tools out of the car and hide them. He also wanted to go get gas. These were little things, of course, but he was itchy to do something, anything, to advance the cause, and with night fast approaching, being itchy about things was about all the action he could take for now.

Oh, and there was one more thing he wanted to do. Suggest to Summer that she make an appointment to get her flying time in. The faster he could get her out of the house, the quicker he could start sabotaging matters and hiding the tools. He was looking forward to standing out there on the bridge, by himself, where he could be immersed in deep thought and run through the plan again and again. He would be able to think about contingencies and cover all the angles without interruption.

Thirty minutes later, they were back at the cabin. Thirty-one minutes later they were both collapsed on the couch sleeping like babies.

FOURTEEN

THE SUN LIT THE CURTAINS like a gentle spark turning into an uncontrolled blaze, as beams of light tiptoed, then marched, broadside,

into the easterly facing room. The couple was clearly under assault, its culprit a solar army that was taking no prisoners.

The evening, which had included a quick midnight retreat to the bedroom, had obviously surrendered.

Summer yawned and arched her body sideways, a crescent moon adorned with gentle female curves and an unrestrainable smile. She could hardly remember the last time she had slept so well and at this moment all felt right with the universe. A vacation from the strains and pressures of the outside world; a wonderful cabin filled with memories, enhanced by fully conscious yet self-delusionary thoughts of a nostalgic utopia; a wonderful husband; and that irrepressible, effervescent feeling that only the first day of a new, yet to be explored trip can bring.

Sure they had arrived yesterday, but everyone knows that the day you land in a new spot on a vacation, is generally a waste. It's like it doesn't count. Not fully at least, marred by travel, acclimation and settling in. It's that first full unblemished day that really starts your vacation. The day when the sky's the limit, the body's completely rested and the saddle sores have been left on the road like discarded trash from fast meals born from a desire to reach one's destination.

And her smile was contagious, to say the least. But only for people awake, which left Hart out of this picture. His eyelids were shut tight as they held on for the dear life of the obviously defeated darkness of the evening that had just passed. The sun was going to win, but not without a good hard fight from Hartence Smith.

Summer looked over at her husband and her smile broadened at his cute little frown. She wanted him to wake up and for a few moments stared at him, willing him to get up. When that didn't work, she considered "accidentally" nudging him with her foot. Maybe she should just let him sleep. Nah.

———————————

Fortified with a hearty breakfast, Hart's typical morning grumpiness had faded and the couple was ready to tackle new frontiers. A nice drive, Cardsdale's Historical Museum, a bit of fishing, a pleasant hike to the falls and a picnic. And then, of course, one not so traditional stop— buying some underwear for Hart. He was tired of going commando. It was all on the agenda, if they could fit it in. If not, there was always tomorrow. Or the next day. Clocks and calendars would have no place on this trip.

Hart pushed himself away from the table. "Summer, that was delicious. Where'd you learn to cook like that?"

"Oh, my Aunt Jemima taught me. And, of course, Mrs. Buttersworth," Summer said with a smile.

"Well, those chicks knew what they were doing.

The eggs and sausage were great, too."

"Thanks, Hart. Glad you liked everything." She reached for his plate.

"No, that's okay. Why don't you go get ready? I'll clean everything up."

Summer smiled. "Thanks, Honey. Actually, could you just put everything in the sink? I'll wash everything before we leave." Then she kissed him and headed down the hall to the bathroom.

The moment he heard the bathroom door close, Hart leaped to his feet. Having already gotten dressed while Summer had cooked breakfast, he beelined for the front door, blowing past it and shutting it without a sound. When he got to his car, he reached into his pocket. "Dammit!" he said out loud as he turned on his heels back toward the house. A distinct feeling came over him that he shouldn't run, yet he didn't want to move too slowly, either. Grabbing the knob on the front door, he exhaled. *Relax.*

It jiggled, but the knob wouldn't turn. "Shit!" *Duh! If I don't have the keys to my car, I'm not going to have them for the house.*

Hart looked in the air and put his hands face up and growled. Then he knocked on the door. He had no choice. Then he knocked louder.

Summer's makeup was half on when she opened the door. She looked at him a little surprised.

Hart's head was down as he nudged past her. "I forgot my keys," he grumbled.

"Oh, that's okay. What were you doing out there?" Her tone was strictly inquisitive.

"Nothing," he said, walking toward the bedroom. She followed a few steps behind him, heading straight for the bathroom. "I just wanted to sit on the porch."

Then he called from the bedroom. "Summer, where the hell are my keys?"

"Did you try your pants pockets?" she called from the bathroom.

My pants pockets? What's the matter with her? "Honey, if they were in my pants pocket, I wouldn't have knocked on the door." *You dipshit.*

"I mean the ones from last night."

"Oh."

With his keys in hand, Hart went whipping past the bathroom door.

"What's the hurry, Hart?"

"Nothing."

"Well, try to relax. We're on vacation."

"Okay," he said, slowing down a bit. "I'm almost done, by the way."

Hart closed the front door behind him gently. Sprinting to his car, he unlocked the car's trunk with his remote as he ran. He grabbed the cable cutters and the rope he had brought with him. His eyes darted around looking for a place to put everything. He couldn't take a chance that Summer would come across this stuff in the trunk.

Then he bolted around the outside of the house, his eyes scanning the scene. He saw the light on in the bathroom. She'd be done soon. He noticed some boulders, but they didn't feel right. Those bushes? Maybe. The shed? Perfect. He turned around and headed straight for it, wondering if she'd be able to see him from the bathroom window. He doubted she'd ever go in there, and even if she did, some bolt cutters and rope would never arouse any suspicion. Not in a shed.

Hart once again got that same feeling at the shed door that he had gotten at the cabin door just a few minutes earlier. Locked. He flung his neck back and growled in frustration. "Dammit!" he whispered to himself.

Then his eyes widened as he remembered something. He reached into his pocket and took out his keys. On the same ring with the key to the front door was a small key for a padlock. Bingo.

––––––––––

After dumping the stuff in the shed, Hart speed- walked back to the front door of the cabin. Reaching for the knob, he wondered if it would be locked. No matter. He had the key now. He opened the door and stepped inside, practically knocking his wife over in the process.

They both pulled back for a moment, exchanging "whoops" and "ohs" and involuntary nervous laughter with each other.

"What's going on?" she said. "Didn't you hear me calling you?"

"No, no. Just jogging around."

She looked a little perplexed. "Anyway. You ready to go?"

"Yeah, sure."

They both noticed the uncleared breakfast table. "Sorry. I promise I'll get to it when we get back," he said.

"No, it's okay. It'll drive me crazy knowing all that stuff's out. You go brush your teeth and I'll clean it up."

"It's all right. I'll clean it up. It's my fault." He made a move for the table.

"Honey," she said, her lips landing on the side of his face. "Trust me, go brush your teeth. There's a reason I'm kissing you on the *cheek*." Then she laughed.

He managed a little laugh himself. Then his lips curled up in a sheepish yet amused smile. *I'm going to miss her.*

FIFTEEN

HART HAD JUST OPENED her door, let her in and was walking toward his side of the car. As she watched him, she had to smile. This vacation was just what she needed. She felt so relaxed. It seemed like a dream. It made her feel like she could do anything, even get pregnant now. The key was to just let it happen. It would take as long as it would take. One month, two months, ten—what difference did it make? In the long run they would have their baby. She and Hart. The key was to enjoy. Enjoy it all. Life's up and downs. And Hart, he had been so wonderful lately. Imagine when I'm pregnant, she thought. He's going to treat me like a queen.

Summer reached over and unlocked Hart's door just before he flung it open.

"Ahh, your timing's impeccable, Summer," he said.

"Well, so is yours."

"What do you mean?" Hart started the car and began driving down the gravelly driveway.

"Don't you remember all those guys who wanted to marry me? You got me just in time," she said with a playful smile.

"Well, you're the lucky one. I saved you."

"Please."

"Nothing but a bunch of horse-faced losers."

Summer laughed. "They were good looking guys and nice."

"Now it's my turn to say, 'Please.' And those names. Larry Break."

"What?"

"You could have ended up Mrs. Summer Break. Oh, and don't forget Percy Vacation. You could have been named Summer Vacation."

"Shut up," Summer laughed.

"It's embarrassing. And don't forget about Roger Picnic."

"And Mortimer School," she added. "And Jerry Camp. He was crazy about me."

"Ooh, that Jerry Camp. I hated that guy. Summer Camp. Yeah I really saved your ass," Hart chuckled.

Summer laughed, then scoffed. "Saved me? Hey, you're lucky my dad even let me marry you at all."

"Yeah, he hated me."

"Well, I don't know if I'd say hate. But I guess he wasn't too crazy about you. Probably the way you always told him he had no dramatic flair."

"Yeah, he was pretty touchy."

"And a keen judge of character."

Hart flashed her a look that made her laugh.

The tires screeched as they went around a curve. "Hart, please slow down. It's beautiful up here.

Let's enjoy the scenery."

Hart let up on the gas and they both looked out the window in silence for a moment.

"You know I really miss him," she said, breaking the silence.

"Who?"

"My dad. And my mom. Everybody. I guess that's why I really want a family of my own. None of mine is really left."

"What about your cousin, what's-her-name?"

"Brandy? We're not very close."

Hart patted her leg. "I'm sure everything's going to work out fine."

"Thanks." Summer smiled.

Hart lowered the windows. "There's Huncke's up ahead. I gotta get gas."

He took his right hand off the steering wheel and clenched and unclenched it a few times.

"Oh, I'm sorry," said Summer. "Do you want me to drive, Honey? You're on vacation. You shouldn't have to drive."

"I'm fine, Sweetie."

Hart would have loved to turn the wheel over to someone else for awhile. And if all went well at the bridge in a few days, he'd never have to drive again—at least not professionally. Which reminded him: "What's going on with your flying lessons?"

"Oh, I booked some time on Thursday up in Apple Grove."

Hart glanced at her. He was starting to feel anxious. Thursday. Two days from now. By Friday he'd be free.

SIXTEEN

HART PULLED INTO HUNCKE'S, adjacent to one of the pump islands and walked toward the register inside the mini-mart.

"Morning." It was Whitman, the man Hart had met earlier when he had first arrived in town to grab some snacks and groceries.

"Hey," said Hart, gesturing upward with his chin. "Fill-up on number, uhh…" Hart looked over his shoulder and then moved toward the door to get a better look. "I can't see it from here," he said bobbing and weaving like a boxer, looking for an opening.

Following his lead, Whitman, staying behind the counter, walked to the end of it and took a look. "The Acura?"

"Yeah."

Whitman hit his forehead with the palm of his hand. "Must be. It's the only car out there," he said mumbling and shaking his head a bit at the superfluousness of his comment.

"That your wife out there?" Whitman asked, squinting and putting up his hand above his eyebrows. He accepted Hart's credit card.

"Uh, yeah, yeah. That's the little woman—with the big mouth."

Whitman laughed causing Hart to smile, but right away he felt self-conscious—given the circumstances. Hart put up his hand. "Just kidding, of course.

She's a doll. Wouldn't trade her for anything."

"Now wait a minute. You haven't heard my offer yet," said Whitman, exploding in laughter.

Hart threw him a courtesy laugh and waved his finger at the man. "Good one, good one," he said as he backed out of the little store as quickly as he could without appearing to be rude.

Hart's perfunctory smile faded as he turned on his heels and headed back to the car, grabbed the nozzle and went through the usual pump routine. Then he opened the driver's side door. "I'm going to hit the bathroom. Frickin' Aunt Jemima."

Summer chuckled. "Have fun."

Hart put his hand on his stomach. He winced, slammed the car door and headed for the men's room, which according to the sign was around back. The door, however, wasn't the only thud he heard. The jarring of the car caused the old sleeveless nozzle to disengage and hit the ground. Hart stopped and turned.

"Shit," he said, bending down and replacing the nozzle, his eyes locked on the slight scratch on the side of his rear panel caused, undoubtedly, by the falling gas nozzle. He sighed and gritted his teeth at the new blemish on his otherwise unmarred car as he walked away, once again to answer nature's call.

Hart could feel his stomach gurgling now as he walked, double-time, to the men's room. Nature's call was becoming a scream. Turning the corner, he oriented himself in a hurry. Ladies' room. Men's room—bingo. He quickly pounded the door open with his balled-up hand, his way of knocking and opening the door at the same time.

He spun to lock the door but found that the old- fashioned thumb screw turned and turned but was obviously broken and would not engage. *Forget it.*

A quick mental survey of the quarters and its prewar fixtures was made as Hart got down to business. After a few minutes he glanced at the lock which at this point was nothing more than decoration. Not his favorite situation, but, oh well, no one seemed to be around anyway.

The Smithsonian Institute should be informed of this place immediately. Those were his last thoughts when he heard the explosion.

SEVENTEEN

NOT NEARLY DONE, Hart scrambled to pull his pants up, the sensation of shaking competing only with the booming noise that was ringing in his ears. His mind groped for answers as vivid, yet purely speculatory, images filled his head. What the hell?

He bolted out the door of the restroom, moving with a restrained and guarded quickness; as fast as he could without running headlong into a danger he knew was there but whose details were completely undefined from his current and blind position.

Peering around the corner, the images in his head morphed into the images that were in fact objective reality. His beautiful car—and everything in it—had been torn apart, burning wreckage scattered everywhere. His car seemed to be the nucleus of the explosion—

at least to Hart, who couldn't take his eyes off of it—but its fiery tentacles reached far and wide, flinging flaming auto parts against the walls of Huncke's, into trees, and into the gas pumps which were moments away from becoming tag team tinderboxes ready to finish the job.

Something told him to get the hell out of there, and that's just what he did.

Hart decided to stay off the beaten path. He'd cut through the forest, needing time to think. Maybe there was some advantage to not being seen. He didn't know what that might be right then, but once the genie was out of the bottle, there'd be no recorking it. So better that he work things out on his own without the possibility of anyone being able to contradict whatever scheme he may have to conjure up.

Summer was dead. That much he figured. And now that his original plan was no longer necessary, he'd be a very rich man a little sooner than he thought. Serendipity had smiled on him and whatever he did, he didn't want to be responsible for messing it up.

If nothing else, he needed a story. Why was he so lucky as to not be at the car during the explosion? The bathroom was a certainly plausible, not to mention *true*, alibi, to be sure. He just wished now that he had asked Whitman where the bathroom was. Get it on record. But it probably didn't matter. It wasn't like some incendiary device would be found at the scene. At least he didn't think one would be. It seemed unlikely that someone blew up the joint on purpose. Of course, if anything fishy was found, he was sure he'd be a prime suspect.

Reaching for a tree branch, he almost slipped as he heard another explosion echoing minutes behind him. This was soon followed by two more. That should be the rest of the pumps, he thought. What a mess. He paused to look at the sky which was now filled with black clouds. They seemed to obstruct the ambient light, making things seem even darker.

Using the location of the sun as a guide, Hart thought himself the true boy scout as he attempted to make his way back to the cabin. Of course the fact that the road was within a hundred yards of him helped tremendously as well.

His goal was a simple one: get back to the cabin before dark. The problem was he wasn't quite sure *why* that was his goal. When his plan regarding Summer's demise had first been hatched, if nothing else, he had felt in control. It may not have been the perfect plan— perhaps unnecessarily elaborate even—but it was *his* plan. The details were his. They were workable. But now, things were different. What had happened to Summer was out of his grasp. He didn't know the whole story and it scared the hell out of him.

But maybe his bewilderment was a good thing. If questioned, he could truthfully, and therefore convincingly, plead ignorance. Why then did he leave? If he was so innocent, why flee the scene, so to speak? Why not stay and help his wife? He wondered if he should go back to Huncke's.

EIGHTEEN

HART STARED AT THE giant pine that loomed over him. He felt a buzzing in his head. He was no longer moving. He had to come up with something. He needed a story, but he felt blocked.

He let his head drop forward, his brow grazing the sturdy tree. And then in one quick motion he spiraled down, twisting his body so that his back landed at the base of the tree. And there he sat, picking at the grass, staring straight ahead, blinking only when necessary. Finally, his forehead crinkled and he let a little smile creep onto the lower part of his face.

He realized that he was acting like a criminal. A guilty criminal. He hadn't done anything. Not one thing. Who cared that he had wanted to kill his wife? He *hadn't* killed her—that was the point.

He had to start thinking like an innocent man. After all, he *was* an innocent man. And innocent men don't think this much. They simply tell the truth. *I went to the bathroom, goddammit. So what? You think I killed her? Good for you! Prove it.*

Obviously, they'd have nothing on him because there was nothing on him. The idea emboldened him. But still he felt that buzzing in his head. It was getting louder and he finally focused enough to recognize it. They were sirens. They were fire trucks, of course, but all Hart could see were the cops.

Why did you flee the scene, Mr. Smith? He was back to square one. *Why, Mr. Smith? Why? Because something told me to get the hell out of there, officer.* He couldn't say that.

Hart took a deep breath. *Why? Answer the question, Hart. Answer it right now. If it comes out shitty, so what? No one's here to hear it. You'll fix it.*

And so he blurted out the first thing that came into his head. "The explosion knocked me down, Officer. Down that hill behind the bathroom. I had tears in my eyes and I couldn't see where I was going. I knew my wife, Summer, she had to be dead and I didn't know what to do. No one could survive an explosion like that and I didn't want to see her burning body.

"I screamed and then I ran. I wanted to die myself. And that's when I slipped and I-I banged my head and everything went black. When I woke up I was disoriented and I just ran. I ran as fast I could. I just wanted to get out of there. I was in the middle of the forest and I kept running, hoping I wasn't getting deeper into nowhere. Finally, I found the road and I made it to the cabin. Is she dead? Is she? Oh, my God."

Hart had said it out loud and he had said it fast. He was sweating. He wondered if it sounded melodramatic. Maybe most people would have stayed nearby, waited for the fire to die down. Maybe. But had he done anything illegal? No. Was there any way they could pin a thing on him? He didn't see how.

Hart felt better. His story made sense. Things are crazy during explosions. People run everywhere. It's pandemonium. Everyone knows that. He didn't do anything bad. He just loved his wife so much and was so traumatized, he couldn't bear to see her charred and mangled remains.

———————

So right or wrong, Hart committed to it all. And he headed back in the direction of the cabin.

Having the basic plot in his mind, he refused to "practice" the story again, wanting it to sound fresh should he be forced to tell it. Instead he decided to focus on other things. For the first time he noticed his complete envelopment in the trees. Together they made for a magnificent quilt of browns and greens. Individually, their detail, their texture, had a certain poignancy that transcended far beyond just one's sense of sight.

Hart was surrounded by nature but was also acutely aware of the manmade road that followed him and acted in a peripheral way as his guide. It was his one link to the only world he really knew—civilization.

This clear mental picture, as well as the joy that bubbled up in him at the prospect of the new life that lay ahead, served as a catalyst in his motivation to move forward. It would not, however, be an easy road. His stomachache was back, having taken a temporary respite during the time the weight of the world had been settling on his shoulders.

If only I could find a tree around here somewhere where I could finish my business, he joked to himself, holding his stomach. But his stab at humor only staved off the inevitable for a few moments. Far from ideal, Hart sucked it up and redecorated the base of the first pine tree on his left.

When he was done, he felt surprised that he didn't feel that much better, concluding that he might be getting hungry. He looked back. Huncke's was far behind and way out of sight. As a matter of fact, he couldn't see much of anything other than trees. An endless sea of trees whose only border seemed to be an amorphous road which was seen rather clearly at times and almost "sensed" at others, its visibility highly dependent upon the density of the trees at any given point and the rise and fall of Hart's chosen pathway.

When the road seemed to be hiding, Hart would become more aware of the glint of the sun, whose brightness advanced and retreated in waves, depending on the lay of the trees.

The sun had shifted a fair amount since he had begun his trek, having passed over his head quite a while ago. And soon, thought Hart, it'll be gone.

He yearned for civilization, feeling both anxious and a little melodramatic. After all, he was far from lost and it hadn't been that long. But still, he kept feeling like any moment now he'd see something, a marker, a bend in the road, anything that would announce to him that the cabin was just around the corner.

He looked at his cell phone. *Why did I pick this time, of all times, to forget to charge my phone*, he thought, seeming to have forgotten about the seven-thousand un-forest-related times he had done the same thing.

Oh, well. One more hour should do it. But he had stopped believing himself, having figured that one more hour should have done it, several times before.

NINETEEN

DESPITE HIS ANXIOUSNESS to get back to the cabin, Hart decided to sit down and take a rest. He was worried that he might fall asleep and that when he woke up, it would be dark. But his worries were unfounded as he had too much on his mind to sleep.

He was right about it getting dark, though. The sun was dropping out of sight, the tall trees seeming to hasten its descent.

He decided to speed up a little, his body running on fumes. God was he thirsty.

And then he stopped. He heard rumblings off in the distance. He strained his ears. It sounded like the crackling footfalls of some animal as its paws hit the forest's needle strewn foundation. And then the muffled sounds of speech. Someone was coming.

Hart slowly moved himself sideways to small group of thick and closely-growing trees until he was thoroughly out of sight.

"The Lakers suck this year." It was a man. He was about twenty years old and looked like a college student.

He was talking to another man about the same age. They were walking at a brisk pace and didn't even come close to seeing Hart who was peering around the trees.

Their voices got louder as they moved closer and closer to Hart, their conversation carefree without the slightest hint that someone might be listening.

"They need another superstar, dude. Kobe can't do it all by himself," said the other man.

Hart could feel himself breathing hard. *Why do I feel like a fugitive?* He didn't know. But he did know that his gut told him not to be seen. That his story would somehow be his own if no one knew where he was.

Hart put the key in the lock and turned the knob. There was no reason it shouldn't open but for some reason he had his doubts.

When he got inside the cabin, he made a beeline for the kitchen sink and filled a large glass of water. He downed it, filled it back up and downed it again. Then he stumbled to the couch and collapsed, his chest rising and falling.

It had been almost two hours since he had seen the two hikers in the forest, and the sun was firmly tucked in for the night. It was good to be home— or in the cabin, at least.

After a moment of lying down, Hart began to nod off. A second later, his head snapped forward and shook. He made a gasping sound and sat up straight. He had to know what was happening. He turned on the T.V., shocked by what he heard next.

TWENTY

AS HE EXPECTED, the explosion was all over the local stations. The thing that surprised Hart was that apparently he, himself, was dead.

Two—not one—bodies were found among the burning wreckage, specifically at ground zero, a late model Acura.

Whitman, the current owner of Huncke's convenience store and gas station, had recognized the couple from an earlier meeting a few days prior.

"They seemed like a nice couple. Spoke with them a couple days ago when they came in for some snacks and such," Whitman said into a microphone held in front of him.

Then the mike was flicked back toward the reporter, a nicely dressed woman, mid-thirties with a flapper-style hat. "Do you have any idea, Mr. Whitman, who they are or where they were staying?"

"Well, as you can see, everything here was destroyed but I do remember their names from his credit card. A joint account, I guess. Hartence Smith, the Third and her name was, uh, Summer. Smith too, I think."

The reporter turned toward the camera. "Well that should be helpful, as apparently the bodies were mangled beyond recognition. Even the teeth in both victims were just obliterated to dust, I've been told. Teeth being something forensic scientists often use to identify victims in such situations. Horrible, horrible tragedy."

Angling toward Whitman, she placed her hand on his shoulder and inquired again, in a confirming manner, if he had any information about where the couple might be staying. Hart perked up. Whitman said he had no idea about anything else and that he had already told the police everything he knew.

As the reporter began to talk again, Whitman stuck his face toward the microphone. "They should check his credit card records. Maybe they— the sheriff can see which motel they were staying in."

Hart couldn't believe it. *Who the hell was that other guy in the car with Summer?*

"I gotta call Brandy. Shit!" he said, remembering his dead phone. Then he ran into the bedroom to get a charger. After tearing apart his suitcase and his chest of drawers, he realized that he had forgotten his charger at home.

"Shit!"

He needed his phone. The cabin had no service. And then he remembered who he had gone on this trip with. Summer always remembered stuff like that. He checked her dresser and sure enough, Miss Organized had brought a charger along. He plugged his phone in and ran back to the T.V.

As expected, all the stations were reporting the same thing. Two bodies. A male and female.

Hart's mind was working overtime. He couldn't decide if this was a blessing or a curse. He didn't have to worry about Summer anymore. He was now a millionaire. An *ex*-trucker. But who the hell was that other guy? There had to be an investigation. Before he went to the cops or the insurance company, he wanted some answers. His biggest fear was that he was somehow overlooking something and that if he did anything rash it might bite him in the ass later.

He had to talk to Brandy. She was the only one he could trust. But that would have to wait until his phone charged.

With nothing left to do for now, Hart made some food and planted himself in front of the television. He jogged around the dial until his "remote finger" was ready to fall off. It was the same news over and over but he couldn't get enough. Finally, he fell asleep, Whitman's interview burned into his brain.

For the second time in a few hours, Hart woke up with a start, gasping. He had been dreaming about explosions. His thoughts were unsettled, feeling like he had gotten drunk halfway through a movie and was completely unsure how things had turned out. The storyline was hazy and seemed to lack finality. Who the hell was that other man in the car? This was no movie. He had to play things right. If he did, he'd be a millionaire, if not, well, God only knew what would happen to him.

All at once, a feeling came over him. He didn't want to be alone. His mouth was dry and he ambled over to the kitchen for a drink of water. Then he looked at his phone. Three bars. Plenty for now. He called Brandy, holding the phone tightly to his head. He began pacing.

"Hart?"

It was her. He felt such relief at hearing her voice. It was nothing. Just Brandy saying his name. But in that context, it felt like a warm blanket. And the feeling of solitude melted away. He stopped pacing, instead resting his elbows on the kitchen counter. He clutched the phone, feeling the impending reassurance he knew was about to overcome him. He was no longer alone.

"Yeah, it's me, Baby."

"Oh my God! I was afraid you were dead. I've been listening to the news and was just too scared to call you."

"You did the right thing," he said. "God, it's great to hear your voice. I have missed you so much."

"I'm so glad you're okay, Hart. I love you so much."

"I love you, too, Baby. I can't wait to see you."

"Me, too."

"We just have to play this the right way and we're home free. It's going to be great."

Brandy sighed happily.

"I'm going to kiss you all over when I see you," Hart said, smiling.

"And I'm going to let you. And then—"

"Wait! I heard something."

Hart strained his ears. Then he heard it again. It was the front door. This time somebody was clearly knocking.

"Shit, the cops. I'll call you back," he whispered, and hung up. As he walked toward the door, his mind raced. Why hadn't he talked to Brandy about what to say to the cops? *Just relax, just relax.*

Hart stood up straight and flung open the door.

Then he turned white.

TWENTY-ONE

SUMMER WATCHED THROUGH the driver's side window as Hart did his double-time walk to the restroom. Poor guy, she thought. *And still no underwear.* She shook her head.

And then she sat very still and listened. She loved the sound of the birds. It seemed to be a constant background, the soundtrack of the forest. And she thought about how easy it was to take it for granted. She wanted to appreciate it all, realizing that that had not always been the case. She was so lucky that her grandmother had a cabin up here. It was the perfect getaway and it really was beautiful.

She looked out the passenger side window, across the road, at the vast valley. It seemed that every square inch was covered and dripping with beauty. Great pines as far as the eye could see. And that soundtrack. That ever-present background melody that gently drove the point home. Nature had thought of everything. And a sudden urge came over her to stretch her legs. She glanced around the car. Cell phone. Purse. Ahh, camera. Flinging her purse to the floor, she stuffed it under her seat, grabbed the camera and jumped out of the car. She was about to slam the door when she remembered the shaky nozzle that was stuck in the gas tank, opting for a gentle close instead.

Then camera in hand, she ran toward the road, looking back only once on the off chance that Hart might emerge. Nope. The only sign of life she saw was Whitman. He was in the store yucking it up on the phone, oblivious to the world around him.

As she ran across the road she wondered if people like Whitman, whom she was sure had lived here forever, no longer saw the beauty of the forest. No longer heard its song. Could be. Maybe it's just human nature.

The road was a two-laner. Sometimes busy, usually not. It was funny, she thought, how these kinds of towns, so isolated, often gave her the creeps. It really was ghost townish. But something about this particular atmosphere gave her a different feeling and she felt overcome by its tranquility. She could finally appreciate why her grandmother liked to get away up here.

On the other side of the road was a relatively small strip of land, nothing exciting. What made it beautiful, however, was its precipitous nature, one of the many natural foyers that overlooked Cardsdale's picturesque valley.

Careful of her footing, Summer stood about five feet from the edge of the drop that lay before her. She took it in for awhile and was soon snapping pictures, thoroughly engrossed and at peace with the world.

Harry Mondran's opportunistic ways had always served him well. Due to other aspects of his nature, however, they would never allow him to thrive, but only to survive. His naturally solid mind had years ago succumbed to the ravages of drugs, alcohol and a generally hard and unsanitary lifestyle. It all seemed to be the result of bad choices, one after another, that snowballed and, in a sense, snuck up on him so gradually that he had never really known what had hit him.

A straight-A student in high school, until his senior year, Harry's upper middleclass upbringing seemed defenseless against a young man who had come to the conclusion that the world was "bullshit" and that there had to be more to life than just getting good grades and taking the traditional path of college, culminating in a boring job, a house in the suburbs, a wife and a couple of kids.

Maybe originally, had he thought in less extreme post-adolescent terms, he might have been able to achieve his goals in a more moderate fashion, but those days were long behind him. He just never seemed to learn the lesson that a party can be fun, but that a party everyday has consequences.

Like an animal, unable to think conceptually, in any meaningful way beyond the present, Harry survived anyway he could now, his plans for a natural existence in some Thoreau-like utopia having died years ago.

Those opportunistic instincts of his, however, were very much alive when he pushed his way through the bushes on that bright and hopeful summer day. He had arrived just in time to see a young woman emerge from a beautiful late-model Acura, closing the door with a certain dainty quality that somehow intrigued him.

Quickly surveying the rest of the scene, Harry liked what he saw. An unattended car, nozzle pumping away with no one in sight. A car so nice the owner's bitch wouldn't even dare slam his doors. Go.

"Come on," he said as he glanced back. Her smile was half-hearted.

"Stelly" Parker loved being with Harry when she was wasted, which it turned out was most of the time. The periods in between getting loaded, however, were often torturous for her. It wasn't Harry that was her problem. She just wasn't much of a go-getter. Even if it involved doing what she had to do in order to score the only thing that made life worthwhile for her.

In the past, this slothful reticence could go on for nearly a week, until the pain became so bad Stelly would resort to almost anything for "a slice of junk," as she called it. When it got to this point, she would become a one-woman trail-blazing ringleader of vice. Desperate and impromptu armed robberies, chain-hooking in feverish twenty-four-hour marathon sessions, brazen snatch-and-grab muggings, you name it. If it wasn't planned out, dripping with mania, and had a high degree of self-destructive risk, it was for her.

That's what was so nice about Harry. He was a steady earner. And he rarely insisted she come along. He brought home the bacon, cooked it and injected it. Usually, she'd hang out at "home" which was nothing more than a lean-to in the woods, but may as well have been the Trump Towers for all she knew most of the time. But this was one of those occasions when she and Harry had ventured off together. A nice little walk in the woods to break the monotony, he had told her. And then back to their little forested sanctuary.

And it was nice. They held hands and talked. She told him again how Hollywood had screwed her over, leaving her nothing but a toothless and desiccated little waif, alone and strung out on those fabled cinematic streets that broke promises, and hearts. And she told him without bitterness, with a smile even. As if because it was a long time ago, it had somehow happened to someone else.

Harry smiled, too, taking simple pleasure in her pleasure. In some crazy way, this cracked shell of a human being gave his life some meaning. It was a horrible existence by most people's standards, but at least he had someone to share it with. Someone who never judged him. Never maligned him. And never made him feel like anything other than her savior, protector and provider.

This being the case, whether by habit or pure coincidence, Harry had led her to the periphery of Huncke's. And when the doorbell rings, dammit, you answer it.

Stelly's smile, already weak, quickly faded all together. She needed desperation to do this. When Harry saw her face, he reached into his back pocket. The flask was three-quarters filled, the top quarter drained on their short walk over. He handed it to her, telling her to hurry. As she tilted her head back, the straight whiskey filled her throat, the burn familiar and comforting.

Harry, meanwhile, took his already lit cigarette from behind his ear—an odd habit he had picked up from his father—and placed it loosely between his lips.

Then he pulled the flask from Stelly's lips, grabbed her hand, and the two of them ran to the car like greedy pirates toward a treasure chest. She muffled her giggles which were nothing more than a manifestation of pure fear.

As they got closer, their hands separated, he bolting toward the driver's side and she toward the passenger's. It was beat the clock and they both knew it.

"Close the door, quietly," Harry said, noticing Summer standing across the street, eyes still soaking up the valley.

Stelly closed the door and began rifling through the glove box, her eyes continuously looking side to side. In contrast, he kept his eyes on his work. If he had to confront someone, he'd deal with it then. He'd become a madman if he had to. No one was going to stop him from taking something he wanted.

"Bingo," he said. Then he nudged Stelly's legs and reached down to where Summer's purse was with one hand, and blindly whipped his cigarette around his back and out the driver's door with the other.

Stelly grabbed for the purse, eager to see what was inside.

Harry closed it. "Later," he said, and they continued to search the car like a pair of honey badgers.

By the time they felt the heat it was too late. The windows were orange, fusing into the rippling air. A partition, a fiery wall of flames, rose like a burning tide, laying siege to the driver's side port. They both pawed at the passenger side door, inadvertently thwarting each other's efforts. But only for a second. All at once they were floating like lotto balls, sucked to and fro into a swirling vapor of heat that instantly melded into an amorphous cloud of gaseous destruction.

The explosion was like a starting pistol that marked Summer's literal slide into the depths of the unknown. Unable to pilot her own body, she felt the air push her as effortlessly as any concrete object may have. In an instant, she was off her feet, whipping randomly as if on a ride that had not been very well thought out, and certainly never checked for safety. She crashed downward into the lip of the cliff's edge. A solid surface true, yet only for a brief moment. Scrambling fingers and fruitless grasping could not save her from the fate once cautioned by the masses to Columbus himself. She'd fallen off the end of the earth.

Her tumble was a brief but scary one, tree branches a blessing and a curse as they both slowed her descent and scratched her at the same time. Like a Pachinko ball, her direction was decidedly downward. How far she'd drop and the exact trajectory of that drop, however, was a complete mystery.

Her screaming, meanwhile, was as non-linear as her fall had been, continuously muffled as her voice caught in her throat each time her ratchety decline suddenly altered direction. Not that her cries would have mattered anyway in the midst of an explosion.

Hitting the ground was a relief, given the circumstances. But only for a moment, as her sense of consciousness cut out just as a battered feeling seemed to permeate her body.

When she woke up, whatever bruises she may have had, seemed to quickly take a back seat to feelings of fear and confusion.

TWENTY-TWO

SUMMER OPENED HER eyes as if time had begun just at that moment, without any feeling of the seconds that had immediately preceded it.

A great sense of calm and precise wariness seemed to overcome her as she embraced the needle-strewn terrain which cradled her prostrated body. *Take it slow and don't panic,* she told herself, resisting the urge to fling her head upward. Hart and I will get through this. An assessment of the situation will be taken, but it will be done slowly and with exactitude, she told herself.

And then the pieces of the puzzle seemed to drift back into her consciousness in a dilatory fashion, the facts organizing themselves mechanically, as brains do.

Within moments, she became aware that Hart was not with her after all. She wondered where he was and if he was okay. She wondered if she'd ever see him again.

As she stood up, she zoned in on what her body had been through. The bumps, the bruises, the soreness. They were readily apparent but miraculously seemed to be minor and she was grateful that everything seemed to be in working order. She had survived, the trees acting, in a sense, like nets that had lowered her to the ground. Roughly, but safely.

The next thing she realized was that she was a long way down from where she had been previously standing. As a matter a fact, as best as she could surmise, she wasn't even *straight* down from where she started. Her path had seemed to veer diagonally, due to the cut of the land, and it became clear that at some point she must have been rolling from one tier down to the next, deeper and deeper into the valley.

"Hello!" she yelled at the top of her lungs. "Hart!"

After calling out several times without so much as an echo in return, she figured she'd better save her energy. She was on her own and it would be getting dark soon— or at least eventually. The thought terrified her and from that point on, the idea of spending the night out here was expelled from her mind. There was no doubt. She would reach her grandmother's cabin by tonight, period.

If there was any silver lining to the situation, it was that the diagonal course that she had tumbled in was at least in the direction of her grandmother's cabin.

She walked along whichever of the valley's tiers she was on, using the sun as her compass, hoping at some point there would be a natural path that would gradually lead upward and out of the heart of the valley.

As she advanced, she tried to be aware of everything around her, her mind at times battling between getting lost in theoretical strategies and speculations, and a real safety-driven need to remain hyper-alert.

One of her biggest problems was the pace with which she would settle upon traveling. Not knowing exactly how far away she was from the cabin and how long it would take, she didn't want to blow all of her energy early on, sapping herself of needed strength later. On the other hand, if she moved too slowly, she might not beat the sun as it lowered itself into the mountainous horizon.

And then she stopped. Even though there was a glaring absence of *Snake X-ing* signs, there it was. Slithering across her path. And taking its sweet time about it, too. Summer put her hand to her mouth and gasped, suppressing the desire to scream her lungs out. She had no idea what kind of snake it was, and didn't care.

"Go. Go," she whispered, waving her arms and dancing in place.

After what felt like half an hour, but was probably only thirty seconds, the snake complied, settling the matter as to how fast Summer would be walking. Double time it was.

After a few hours Summer couldn't help but feel as though she had made great strides—assuming, of course, she was heading in the right direction. She had a slight sense of doubt about this, but all in all, a surprising feeling of confidence had seemed to eclipse fear as her new motivating factor. She would make it back to the cabin and she somehow knew this.

She remembered being lost once at Dodger Stadium when she was about eight years old and how scared she'd been. Would she ever see her parents again? Who knew?—at the time. It's all so hazy and unstable when you don't know the end of the story. But looking back, knowing the ending, makes it a lesson; a bit of strength for the spirit that each of us can carry in our arsenal if we choose to see it that way.

And so it was, with this mindset, that she trucked forward. Grateful that she had survived the fall, her will intact. Thirsty and hungry, she knew that when she would eat and drink later, she could look back at this moment with a certain degree of joy, the full story played out, the ending known.

The fate of Hart was the most difficult of all for her. It was the aspect of the narrative that she had the least control over. She prayed he was okay but that was all she could do for now, pray.

The sun was at her back and sinking fast. Summer hoped she would not have to spend the night out here, but even the prospect of that was accepted with a certain calm that surprised the hell out of her.

An hour later, this bullishness was bolstered even further when she at last saw a way up from the tier on which she had been tramping for the last several hours. It felt exciting that her movement would now be vertical.

As the tiers dovetailed, the slope of each became less severe. This gradual flattening had allowed trees to spring forth, where earlier the lay of the land had been too sheer to permit much growth.

The relative density of the trees would make it possible to scale the walls of the valley as she now had something to hold on to, and so up she went, almost giddy at her new discovery.

She moved from tree to tree with a new sense of vigor fueled by adrenaline and a positive will. Sometimes she almost leaped to the next tree. And when the trees were farther apart, she'd take steps in between like in the triple jump.

The real challenge, of course, was when the span between the trees were spaced at a fairly large distance. When this happened, Summer really had to bear down, clutching rocks and clumps of not-so-established dirt in an effort to avoid sliding back down. Sometimes she'd push herself into the rock wall, feeling herself trembling and gradually losing the battle with gravity.

On one occasion she lost about twenty feet, not to mention some skin. She felt her heart pounding the whole way down and for minutes after. It was at this time that she became aware of the darkening aura that was surrounding her as the sun made its final descent behind the mountains at the other side of the valley.

She hoped the moon would be fairly bright tonight, realizing that she didn't have much by which to gauge it as she hadn't paid much attention to the sky the night before. And even in the light of day she hadn't been able to get a good sense of the moon's size as something had been blocking it whenever she had tried to look.

As she reached the top of the first tier, the feel of the forest had changed and Summer was very much aware of it. The terrain had remained the same, but an altered backdrop had unfurled to accommodate a new act in the play. Darkness was now dominating, but tempered by a haze of light led by a milky swath of stars and more importantly a moon that was thankfully almost full.

TWENTY-THREE

I LOVE YOU, TOO, SWEETHEART. I can't wait to see you." At first Summer thought the words were directed at her. But they made no sense. I love you, too? Too? She hadn't even said anything. I can't wait to see you? Why would you say that to someone who was a few feet away, just outside?

Maybe she hadn't heard right. She was exhausted. Thirsty. Maybe just not thinking clearly. Besides, the words were faint, coming from behind the door.

This last hour had in some ways been the toughest of her trek back to the cottage. Even though the terrain had been relatively flat, this hike had had an attritional effect on Summer that seemed to weigh the heaviest that final hour. The proverbial straw that broke the camel's back.

Her feet were like lead and she had long ago blocked out her bumps and bruises as her desire for water, rest and peace of mind had obscured all else.

When she had seen the light coming from her grandmother's cabin, it felt like one last shot of adrenaline had been injected. *Hart! Hart must be home. He must be safe,* she thought.

And then, "I love you, too, Sweetheart. I can't wait to see you." It was as if Hart had read her mind and answered her before she could speak. Or maybe she had said it. Was she that punch drunk?

Summer stood not quite at the door. For some reason she lingered back a few feet, her body swaying like she was trying to get her sea legs.

Hart continued: "We just have to play this the right way and we're home free. It's going to be great."

Was she dreaming? Who was he talking to? And what was he talking about?

"I'm going to kiss you all over when I see you." That was the next thing she heard. Or thought she heard. And then her hand jetted out and seized the knob of the front door.

"Wait! I heard something," he said.

And before she knew what she was doing, she was knocking.

Then silence. Or shuffling. Maybe whispering. She didn't know what she was hearing. She was ready to faint, she felt so lightheaded. The words she had just heard hung in the air. And as the door felt like it was about to open, she filed them in the back of her brain. They would not be forgotten but would instead be played like an ace—used when most needed, rather than when it would cause the table to fold before its time. And though it surprised her that she was thinking this way, it felt like the most prudent thing to do. After all, maybe she needed more information or maybe, in her semi-delirious and dehydrated state, she had just imagined the whole thing. Maybe she'd wake up any moment now. Or maybe she was fooling herself.

TWENTY-FOUR

HART FLUNG THE DOOR OPEN the way one might tear off an adhesive bandage. He had forced himself to stand up straight. He would face the cops without a hint of guilt or wrongdoing. After all, he hadn't done anything wrong, had he?

But what he saw when he opened the door made the blood drain from his face. A million thoughts flooded his head. But one thought wisely bolted to the forefront of his mind: hug her. He did, as he said her name and other requisite things like, "Thank God you're alive." He actually pulled it off quite well, aided by the emotional aspect of it all bubbling so close to the surface.

Summer was in a daze, but she hugged him back hard, the tears coming easily.

How are you not dead? Hart wanted to scream but composed himself enough to ask it in a way that didn't make himself sound like he was either bitterly disappointed or like some kind of sick maniac.

Hart played the doting husband as he led Summer to the couch and brought her as much water as she needed and tended to her scrapes and cuts.

The relief and comfort she felt could hardly be expressed and she broke down a few times, each episode greeted with warm embraces and comforting words from Hart. He had dramatic flair after all, throwing himself into his part, dying to know what happened—why she wasn't dead, how she'd destroyed his seemingly serendipitous plans— all while treating her with kid gloves.

Hart listened with great interest to Summer as she explained how she was not in the car when she heard the horrible explosion. He sympathized with her when she recounted how she had made it out of the valley and back to the cabin, even managing to diplomatically confirm that she hadn't been seen by a soul. And he, of course, expressed how relieved he was that she was home safe.

All the while, however, behind those commiserating eyes, the wheels turned. He felt like the winning lottery ticket had been yanked out of his hands. She had been out of the picture and now she was back. So the narrative would have to change and he'd have to stay one step ahead of it all if—

"What are you looking at?" Hart asked, interrupting his own thoughts. But they both knew where her eyes were.

"Oh, the phone," he said. Hart had some explaining to do. The phone. He glanced back at it to give it the full effect.

"Oh, I was just talking to your cousin Brandy." And now he was really scrambling, trying to remember what he said; wondering how long Summer had been on the porch before she had knocked; what she might have heard.

"I was worried about you and I just needed someone to talk to," he continued.

"Oh," said Summer. Her thinking was still cloudy so she decided not to question Hart about what she thought she might have heard. For a brief moment she asked herself if she was just trying to avoid a confrontation. If that was the case, it made her feel ashamed, but, no, she didn't think that was it. She just wanted to be on firmer ground before proceeding. But her antenna was definitely up. For the first time in her life she wasn't sure if she could trust Hart.

It just seemed odd that of all people to call, Hart would choose Brandy. I mean she had never been particularly close to her cousin. And Hart certainly never had been either. Or had he?

"Yeah, she's on her way up now," Hart said. "To see if she could help out. Thank God you're okay though. Now it'll be like a little family vacation."

"I'm surprised you even have her number," Summer said, regretting it the moment it came out. She wanted Hart's guard to be down; not wanting him to know she suspected anything.

"Oh, well it was in one of the drawers in the kitchen along with other family numbers. That's why I called her actually."

"So are you going to call her back and tell her I'm alright?"

"Yeah, yeah, I better. I just got so caught up I forgot about her."

He definitely played it well and Summer wasn't sure what to believe. She decided to listen closely, pretend like she wasn't, and see if she'd pick anything up by the way Hart talked and acted.

He walked over to his phone.

"Hart, did you try calling my cell, by the way?" He didn't even hesitate. "Of course. Many times.

There was no answer."

It made sense, seeing as her phone had blown up in the explosion.

From his point of view, of course, his response was a big risk that he could have been called on if Summer did in fact have her phone. On the other hand, actually saying "no" to the question she posed would have been bordered on ridiculous.

"Hi Brandy?" Hart said into the phone. "This is Hart. You're not going to believe this. Summer's alive!" There was a beat and Summer noticed that Hart was smiling from ear to ear. "Yeah, yeah, she wasn't in the car." Hart was nodding and smiling and pacing. "I know, I know, it's unbelievable. Anyway, we'll tell you all about it when you get here...I know. I'm so relieved, too. Thank God she's okay...Okay, you drive safe... We'll see you soon...Bye."

Hart hung up the phone. "She was so relieved. Oh my God. I know you guys were never that close but she was really worried."

Summer, still on the couch, smiled and sipped some water.

"Anyway, she's on her way up," said Hart.

Summer yawned, got up, and headed in the direction of the bedroom. "Well, I guess I'll say 'hi' tomorrow morning. I'm exhausted."

"Good night, Honey," he said, coming over to her and embracing and kissing her.

She returned his embrace and began shuffling toward the bedroom. Then she stopped and turned. "Hart?"

"Yes, Honey?"

"What's going on with the police?"

Hart felt his face flush. "What do you mean?" For the first time tonight, he sounded a little jittery.

"I mean you reported me missing, right? I assume they're out there looking for me."

"Oh. Oh, yeah. I already talked to them after the explosion." He tried to choose his words as carefully as he could while trying to sound like he wasn't thinking too hard.

"They actually drove me home." He felt dumbfounded, being thrust into the main performance without ever having a chance to hear how his lines sounded out loud. Then he figured the less said, the better.

But despite her weariness, Summer just looked at him, gesturing slightly with her hands, clearly waiting for more.

"Well, it feels strange to say this out loud, but, uh, they're not really looking for you because they think you're, you're dead. I mean that you, you blew up in the explosion."

Summer pursed her lips and nodded. "Hmm." It did seem strange hearing that. But it made sense. After all, Hart had thought she was dead. Why not the police? "Well, let's see what the news says. It must be on the –"

She stumbled as she moved toward the coffee table, reaching for the remote. Hart sidled over, trying to appear casual but unavoidably looking awkward in the process.

He clutched the remote. "It's actually broken. I was trying all day."

"Oh," she said.

"Listen, Sweetheart," he said, hugging her. "You've had a long day. I'm worried about you. Why don't you get some sleep, huh? I'll call the police and tell them you're okay. And I'll see if I can get the damn T.V. working."

He held her loosely now and put his forehead against hers and smiled. Then he kissed her. "Get some rest Sweetheart."

She nodded and headed into the bedroom.

TWENTY-FIVE

A SECOND WIND HAD SEEMED to kick in for Summer, no doubt helped along by a warm shower taken in the attached bathroom. She felt tired but no longer sleepy. As she got undressed and ready for bed she felt uneasy. She wished there was a T.V. in the bedroom but that really wouldn't have been Grandma's style. Something wasn't adding up. Something—

The knock was quick. It announced an arrival—a statement, not a question—as the door promptly swung open.

"I brought you some warm milk," Hart said. "Hope it helps you relax so you can get some sleep." Without hesitating, he walked over to her nightstand and put the milk down.

"Thanks, Hart."

He kissed her cheek, said 'goodnight' and left, closing the door behind him.

Summer sat down on the bed and tried to remember what she was thinking about before Hart had come in.

Then she heard a voice. It was Hart's. She tip-toe-ran to the bedroom door and listened.

"…yes, that's right, officer, she's completely okay.

Thank God she wasn't in the car."

Summer opened the door just a little bit and looked out. Hart was talking on the phone, his back turned toward her.

"Thank you so much for all your help…you too, have a great night."

Summer closed the door quietly and headed toward the bathroom to brush and floss her teeth, a ritual she performed almost without fail, no matter how late it was or the circumstances. When she was done, she ambled to her bed, wiped out, yet trying to focus.

She noticed her alarm clock and wondered what time she should get up tomorrow. It was out of habit really. Then she looked at her pillow. *Forget it. I'll get up whenever. I'm exhausted and I'm on vacation for God's sake.*

Turning her head back, she saw the glass of milk. *Oh yeah, the milk. Nah, I already brushed my teeth. Forget it.*

Yawning, she killed the lights and got under the covers. It didn't take long before her eyelids began to lose the gravity war and within moments she was asleep.

Two seconds later, her eyes snapped open and her head flew up, her body following, putting her in the sitting position. *The alarm*, she thought.

Looking at the bedroom door, she slid out of bed and, on her knees, turned the volume down on the alarm clock. Then she turned the radio on and slowly raised the volume up so it could barely be heard. She did not have to flip around the dial long before she found what she wanted.

"...the two bodies that were found in the car that exploded this afternoon at Huncke's Service Station in Cardsdale are disfigured beyond recognition, but are thought to be the remains of Hartence and Summer Smith of San Gabriel. The exact cause of—"

Summer's ear's strained. Sounding like something beyond just the radio, she cut the power and leaped back into bed, pretending to sleep like a little kid afraid of being caught by his parents. She even mumbled a bit in case Hart had heard something. It was quiet but she knew he was there, the gap in the opened door filled by his suspicious eye. Unable to help herself, she opened her eyes. She'd let him know that she was not a sound sleeper.

But when her eyes opened, she saw nothing but darkness. Maybe she was the suspicious one. Maybe.

Feeling around, she almost knocked over the glass of milk. She breathed a sigh of relief when she finally clutched it. She then jog-walked to the bathroom, dumped the milk down the drain and let the water run for almost a minute. Then she returned to bed, replacing the glass on her nightstand.

TWENTY-SIX

HART HAD JUST FINISHED cutting the tiny protruding copper wire on the coaxial cable to the T.V. when Brandy pulled up. A twinge of excitement filled his chest. He was giddy about the idea that he'd now have a live sounding board in order to hash out and finalize his plans. The desire to voice his ideas out loud, with someone who was on the same wavelength, was overwhelming. He wanted to keep his plan foolproof and use every new wrinkle—such as the explosion—to his advantage.

Brandy, for her part, felt a little nervous. She had been eager to share in the spoils of Summer's demise, but not so eager to actually be involved, and almost as paramountly not be *perceived* to be involved in any way.

It was for this reason that she felt some relief at having driven up to the cabin in the dead of night. Without a living soul on the road, not even any passing headlights, her apprehension was somewhat mollified by the idea that no one knew she was here. All in all, she couldn't wait until the whole matter was settled.

One consolation, she told herself, was that by being here she'd be better able to direct Hart, helping to make sure he didn't foul things up.

Brandy entered the cabin and greeted Hart. They hugged, with Hart holding on a little too long, going so far as to nibble on her ear. She pried him away as subtly as she could.

"Where's Summer," she whispered. "It's okay, she's sleeping."

"Good. But take it easy. We don't want to be stupid here. You're almost home free."

Hart shrugged and nodded in agreement. He knew she was right but that didn't stop his excitement from spilling over into a confidence that made the whole scheme a possibility in the first place. He also had trouble with the idea that Brandy would suspect for a moment that he wasn't up to the task.

Then Hart made a face. "What's that perfume you're wearing? Is it new?"

"Why?"

"Because it—" He closed his eyes and exhaled hard a few times. Then he sneezed. And not softly.

They both looked toward the bedroom door.

"I better check to see if she's awake," Summer heard Hart say through the door.

She closed her eyes as the door to her room was cracked open. Hart only looked for a moment before shutting the door as quietly as he could.

Then he turned to Brandy. "She's asleep. I wouldn't worry. She's exhausted. I even gave her some warm milk before she hit the hay."

"Maybe we should discuss our plans later."

"When?" he said, hissing a bit. "We gotta get this settled and after tonight when are we gonna have a chance to be alone without looking suspicious."

"Okay, okay," she said, whispering at an especially low volume.

"Let's go outside if it'll make you feel better."

"It's cold out there."

Hart threw up his hands and was about to open his mouth.

Brandy rolled her eyes. "Alright, let's go outside.

I'll put on a jacket. But talk fast."

Closing the front door behind them softly, Hart started talking first.

"Beautiful night."

"Come on, Hart."

"Hey, if you're cold, lemme put my arms around you."

"Don't be stupid. There's plenty of time for that. Now tell me what's going on."

Hart smirked. "Alright. First of all, Summer has no idea what's going on. She knows my car blew up but has no clue that two people died in the explosion. We're gonna use that to our advantage. After we take care of Summer, I'm going to go to the cops and tell them how I was lost in the woods for a few days and that's why I waited until now to come to them."

"Okay, but they're going to ask why you were in the woods."

"I was lost there."

"Hart, focus. There's an explosion. Where were you? Why weren't you in the car? I mean how'd you get in the woods in the first place?"

"Oh." He sighed. "That's why I'm glad I'm talking to you, so we can hash this out, out loud."

They were quiet for moment, both thinking.

"Wait a minute," Brandy said. "How did Summer survive? Why wasn't she in the car? Maybe that could be *your* story."

"Huh. Yeah, that's good. She was, uh—she told me she was looking out over the valley and the explosion knocked her off the edge. Yeah, that's totally believable because it really happened."

"Perfect. So you were lost in the woods, down in the valley for a few days. You took a look while the car was gassing up and she was in the car when it blew up."

"Yeah. Good," he said.

"By the way, where were you really when it blew up?"

"What's the difference?"

She looked at him furrowing her brow. "Well come on, tell me. What's the big deal."

"I was in the john, okay?"

She smiled. "I gotta hand it to you—you have dramatic flair."

"Yeah, well it saved my life, so…"

"Alright, next question. Who was the second body they found?"

"I've been thinking about that. I think I'm going to tell the cops that I really don't know but it might have been this homeless guy I saw once hanging around the gas station. Maybe he was hitting Summer up for some money."

"That's not bad. And you know it's really not up to you to figure out who that second body was anyway.

You just play dumb. You know the second body's not you. You're surprised as hell that there even is a second body."

"Yeah, but still I think it's a good idea to let the cops know that there's uh, a reasonable reason for the second guy," Hart said.

"Yeah, just don't press it too much. Remember you just got out of the woods, you don't know what the hell's going on, you're upset that your wife is dead and you're not trying to solve a case and come up with theories because you don't even care who the other body is. You're too upset about your wife."

"I'm just saying that it wouldn't hurt to give them an idea."

Alright, Columbo. "Fine," she said, feeling an unnecessary fight coming on. Then, unable to help herself, she added, "Just don't come off as suspicious."

"Hey, I know how to handle things, alright?"

"Fine, fine, let's move on."

"And you know, *you* asked me who the second body was supposed to be."

"For *us*, Hart. Not for the cops. Let them speculate themselves. Alright forget it, forget it. It doesn't matter. Let's move on."

"You brought it up," he muttered under his breath. "Alright, so what about the plan?"

"I hid the extra rope and bolt cutters in the shed. Tomorrow, I'll take a walk by myself. You and what's her name do some girl stuff, just the two of you."

Brandy rolled her eyes. "What Hart, like a pillow fight in our bras and panties?"

"That sounds good. Just make sure you videotape

it. Anyway, keep her busy. I know how much you two have in common."

Brandy clenched her lips. *Girl stuff,* she scoffed. "Okay, so I hide the bolt cutters on the other side of the bridge and tie the rope to the bridge so I can pull it up later after Summer's accident."

"Sounds good. Now let's go in. I'm freezing."

Hart gestured toward her chest. "You don't look that cold to me."

Brandy half-smiled, amused but annoyed, and slapped his hand away.

"Come on let's go in. I'm cold."

He smiled and reached out again as she turned away, hugging her chest. "Take my word for it," she said. "Alright, hold on," he said. "We gotta go through the rest of the plan."

"We've been over it, Hart."

"Hey, I need to say it out loud, make sure it all makes sense. Now try to focus, will you?"

She wanted to say she was cold again, but took the path of least resistance and assumed a serious look on her face. "Alright, go ahead."

"Okay, we take a walk across the bridge. Me first. I tell Summer I forgot my gloves back where we just were before crossing the bridge. She'll go and get them for me and I'll keep moving ahead to the other side of the bridge. She gets my gloves, comes across the bridge. When she's halfway across, I cut the bridge's ropes. Bye-bye Summer. The cops won't even be looking for her since she died in that horrible explosion. Come on, let's go to the back seat of your car and celebrate."

Hart said that last line so fast, Brandy had to laugh.

Then he grabbed her hand and started walking toward her car. Her resistance was flirtatious and half-hearted.

Summer pulled away from the inside of the cabin door and walked quickly, but quietly back to the bedroom. She closed the door without a sound and leaped on her bed. She buried her head in her pillow.

She had played it well and gotten her confirmation. Any doubts, any initial denials were gone for good. She felt dumb that she had even questioned herself.

She waited to hear the front door. Silence. She guessed they did go to Brandy's car. *Brandy. My cousin.* Her mind was whizzing at top speed. Tears, anger, exhaustion. It was happening all at once and she could have thought about it all night but her battered body wouldn't let her.

Within minutes, she was asleep again. This time with the unimaginable knowledge that her own husband was going to kill her.

TWENTY-SEVEN

THE NEXT DAY, SUMMER woke up late. She had slept a long time but it wasn't very restful as she tossed and turned most of the night. At one point in the evening she became aware that Hart had come to bed and was lying next to her.

But when she looked over this morning, she felt relieved to see that he was gone. She glanced toward the bathroom. It was empty. Good. It would give her a chance to collect herself and figure out what she was going to do.

She sighed. She felt very sad, but chose to deal with the pain later. This was pretty unusual for her. As a matter of fact, Hart had frequently admonished her over the years for coming unglued. He would tell her to always relax when you have a problem.

Remain calm and take quiet action. This time she would take his advice.

After staring at the ceiling for a few moments, Summer made herself get out of bed. Then she used the bathroom and got dressed.

Looking for an excuse to stay in the bedroom, she looked around the room and saw that Hart's shorts were on the floor. No great surprise there. She remembered the fact that he had forgotten to pack his underwear which didn't seem all that cute to her anymore.

Picking up his shorts, as she always did, she noticed that they had a little weight to them on one side. It was his cell phone, left in his pocket. Not thinking much about it, she was going to put the shorts in the drawer, a habit consistent with what she usually did at home, when she stopped herself and took out the phone. It was so against her nature to snoop on someone else's phone— even though his true character had been revealed—that she felt odd.

As she scrolled down, the first thing she noticed was the numerous calls back and forth between Hart and Brandy. Then she checked for Hart's call to the police last night. Never happened.

It was nothing to get upset about she told herself.

Just more confirmation.

———————————

When she opened the bedroom door she wasn't sure what to expect.

"Hey sleepyhead." It was Brandy, who came toward her, all smiles. Brandy threw her arms around Summer and squeezed her warmly. Summer hugged her back.

When their embrace broke, Brandy looked at Summer so intensely, Summer felt like she had to look away but didn't allow herself to.

"How are you doing?" Brandy said. "I heard about your horrible experience in the woods. Thank God you're okay."

The women made their way to the couch.

"Oh, I'm a little shook up but I'll be okay." As she said it, Summer felt good, immediately recognizing that after her disquieting experience in the woods, if she seemed out of it she'd have a good excuse.

Then she looked around. "Where's Hart?"

"Oh, he decided to take a walk," said Brandy.

Summer realized at that moment that it would be hard to see Hart. And even harder to see him with Brandy.

———————————

The cousins continued to engage in small talk as Summer finished her breakfast. When they ran out of things to discuss, one of them would mention something about Grandma or a childhood memory. There were even moments of laughter, each wondering if the other was sincere in her merriment.

"It was so nice of you to come up," Summer said. "I know we haven't always been that close. Is it a problem at all getting away from work?"

"No, I had already told them I was taking some time off and started driving up toward Cardsdale a few days ago." She stopped and turned a little pale. *A few days ago?* Maybe she had gotten a little too comfortable; let her guard down. She looked at Summer but had trouble reading her face and so immediately tried to play it off, pretend nothing was up and change the subject.

"Yeah," Brandy continued, laughing. "And would you believe I missed the off-ramp for my favorite motel.

I was so tired I just slept in the car. The next day I ate some food I had brought along, read a book and splashed my feet in the creek. It was kind of strange because no one else was around. It's weird not seeing a single person around for two whole days. You think Cardsdale's a small town, you should see some of the places along the way. Nobody. And then I heard about the explosion in Cardsdale and got a call from Hart a little while later and he thought you were dead. Oh, my God, it was crazy. But thank God you're okay."

It was hard not to notice how fast Brandy was talking but Summer didn't say anything or react in any way that might seem unusual. She also didn't ask why Brandy was heading toward Cardsdale in the first place or why Hart would call her— obviously the story about Grandma keeping Brandy's phone number in a drawer in the cabin was a bunch of crap. But no, Summer wouldn't try to trip anyone up. The more she played it cool, the more she learned the truth. If she had any advantage, it was that they didn't know that she knew.

When Hart returned from his walk, Summer had trouble looking him in the eye, but forced herself to do so. Seeing Hart and Brandy in the same room made it twice as bad. At one point she felt herself tearing up and wanted to run from the room. Hart saw her face.

"Come on, Summer, take it easy. There's nothing worth falling apart about. You're back now and you're safe. I know it was tough out there in the woods by yourself."

"Yeah, you're right. Maybe I just need to be alone for a while."

Summer headed for the door.

"Where you going?" asked Hart, moving toward her.

"I thought I'd just go take a walk."

"Uh, you mean on Grandma's property, or uh, where, where?" If she was seen by anyone, his plan would be screwed.

Summer felt tempted to ask him why he was acting so nervous, but didn't. "Uh just on Grandma's property."

"All right, have a nice time."

TWENTY-EIGHT

THE MOMENT SHE LEFT the cabin, the waterworks came on. She was so incredibly sad and felt a terrible pain in her chest. She hadn't felt heartache like this for God knows how long. It was like a horrible break-up or like losing a loved one. She just wanted to cry and never stop. What was she going to do?

When she reached the bridge, she paused. Looking at it and the gorge below felt surreal, like she was at a crime scene. A murder scene. Hers.

She walked onto the bridge and felt surprised. She was scared but in a different way from before. It was hard to explain to herself and she didn't try.

When she reached the midpoint, she stopped and looked straight out at the gorge. Then she looked down. Tears fell from her eyes and into the gorge like wispy flakes of snow that would surely dissolve into nothing before hitting the vast depths of darkness below. It was a hell of a drop any way you slice it. And it was right there that she thought about jumping.

After a few moments she meandered down the bridge and as she walked, she looked at its construction; how it was built, the detail. Actually, it wasn't all that complicated. Strong, but simple in design. When she reached the other side she looked back. After staring at the bridge for a while, she continued walking a few steps before sitting down on a boulder that was close by.

It wasn't long before she noticed something at the base of a nearby tree. Whatever it was seemed to be covered with a bush whose tiny "trunk" appeared to be held down by a twenty, twenty-five-pound rock. She walked toward the tree out of curiosity but didn't get more than two feet before she figured out what it was. It was a rope. It was tied to the bottom of the tree and trailed away toward the bridge.

The part of the rope that was on the ground was covered by dirt and pine needles to camouflage its presence and could not really be seen unless one was looking for it. Another part of the rope, the part that emerged from under the bridge ran straight for a while before being coiled up and hidden behind some bushes. The coil was loosely wound and appeared to be extremely long. It was all related to the part of the plan that was going to allow Hart to reel up the bridge after he cut it.

As she walked back toward the bridge Summer noticed something else. Due to the angle, this object could only be seen from this side of the bridge. The bolt cutters. There they were, right near the bridge's anchor, covered almost completely by a leafy plant.

She walked toward the cutting tool, completely unsure what she'd do when she got to it.

TWENTY-NINE

AS SUMMER ENTERED the cabin she half expected to see Hart and Brandy in the throes of passion. Another thing she suspected was that soon, probably today or tomorrow, Hart was going to ask her to go for a walk.

If there had been any throes of passion, they had ceased. As for the walk, Hart didn't waste much time bringing it up.

"I just got *back* from a walk, Hart," Summer said. "I know. I know. I mean later. Maybe early evening."

And then possibly as a way of coaxing her into it after seeing her reaction, Hart decided to play the camping card. "Maybe we could make it a hike and then all go camping for a day or two. That would be different, rough it for a few days."

That was the camping card. If Summer wasn't too hot on a walk, she would be even less enthused about going for a hike and about camping out. Based on her history, Hart figured, camping should scare her enough that a simple walk, even if it was over the bridge, would seem tame by comparison.

And the reality was that Hart was feeling a little anxious. He wanted to get this over with and also didn't want too many days to go by before he would talk to the police and claim that he had been lost in the woods. The longer he waited, he reasoned, the less believable it would all seem.

"I don't know, maybe. I'm a little tired right now. I'm going to take a little nap," Summer replied as she made her way to the bedroom.

She closed the door and Hart and Brandy looked at each other.

Summer got undressed down to her underwear and slipped into bed. She stared up at the ceiling and made pictures in her mind out of the wood grains and knots that decorated the planks above.

The ceiling was vaulted, maybe fifteen to twenty feet high. And she imagined herself falling from it, over and over again, onto the bed. *That* would be jarring. Imagine the gorge.

And then the image got blurry, clouded by a watery glaze that filled her eyes, until she'd blink and feel the cool, cool trails that meandered down her temples, filling and damming her ears.

After an hour had passed, she was all cried out. And ready.

Summer emerged from the bedroom dressed in sweats. There was a look of tranquility about her.

Hart was on the couch thumbing through a magazine, unable to settle on any one page and Brandy was over at the dining table playing solitaire.

"Look what I found in Grandma's closet," Summer said. It was a backpack.

Hart and Brandy looked up. "What's that for?" asked Hart.

"It's for camping. And I remember my Grandmother kept most of the other equipment in the other room."

"Oh," said Hart, really turning his body toward Summer now. "So you want to go camping?"

"Yeah, that's what you said, right?" Brandy looked at Hart.

"Uh, yeah, yeah, great. Tonight?" he asked. "Sounds good. Why don't we eat and then we can pack up and go before it gets dark."

Hart stuck his bottom lip out. "Okay."

Summer moved toward the kitchen. "Sandwiches okay with everyone?"

Brandy and Hart agreed and Hart went into the other room and came out with some camping supplies. "Look what I found—a couple of backpacks." Summer looked up, half-smiled and went back to making the sandwiches. Then Hart looked at Brandy.

"Hart," Brandy said, her teeth a little clenched. "Remember I said that I didn't want to go? Too many cooks in the kitchen? You two just go. Three's a crowd."

Hart smirked. "Got any other clichés you wish to share? How about camping loves company?"

Fuck you, she mouthed to Hart, peeking over at Summer to make sure she wasn't watching.

Hart smiled. "What about, 'Tis better to have camped and, uh…roasted marshmallows than to never have camped before."

Summer chuckled and then said, "Hart, if she doesn't want to go then leave her alone."

"You know, it's funny, when you were taking a nap, Brandy told me how much she loves camping and how you were always the one who never wanted to go when you were a kid. Now you want to go and Brandy doesn't. What a fuckin' crazy family."

Hart paused for a moment and then changed his tone.

"Look, we all should go. There's too much to take and I just think we all need a little R and R. So Brandy, just help us out, please. You don't need a backpack. You can just carry the tent. It's pretty light. Come on, we need you and it'll be fun. You're our guest here. We should do things together."

Brandy squeezed her lips together and cocked her head a little. "Okay, Hart." Then she glanced up at Summer and quickly looked away.

Hart and Brandy finished getting their stuff together and convened in the living room.

"How you doing in there?" Hart called to Summer, still in the bedroom.

"I'll be ready in a couple minutes."

Hart and Brandy had been avoiding eye contact but looked at each other at the same time when they realized that they would be alone for a few minutes. "You son of a bitch," she hissed.

"Hey, screw you, Brandy," Hart said, clutching her arm and leading her toward the front door. "You're just as much a part of this as I am."

They were both careful to whisper.

Brandy looked toward the bedroom door. "Hey, I never wanted to kill her."

Hart's eyes opened wide and he gaped at her. "It was your idea, you dumb bitch."

"Yeah, but that doesn't mean I want to be there when it happens, asshole," she said spitting air at him.

His voice got a little louder. "Oh no, you just want the rewards. You want *me* to do all the heavy lifting."

"Shhh. Hey, we already worked things out. That's what we agreed to, jerkoff."

"Yeah, well things changed. So roll with it."

"Hey listen, if—"

"Ready to go." It was Summer. She was standing at the bedroom door, backpack in tow.

THIRTY

A S THE THREE OF THEM began the hike, it was apparent that there was at least a little tension in the air.

Hart was deep in thought about his impending task. Two things were important to him. One was that he would be successful. The second was that he would handle things well. He wanted to be a certain kind of guy. A big fish. He had planned this thing out and had been handed a real gift in that everyone already thought Summer was dead, giving him the perfect alibi He wanted to carry his plan out with a certain flair that said, 'You're unique. You're not like everyone else. You beat the system. You, Hartence Smith the Third, don't shoot people in the back. You draw, spin your gun around, do a cartwheel, and *then* outdraw your nemesis. You do it with panache, if that's the right word. I'm pretty sure it is.'

That's what he had been trying to get Brandy to understand from the beginning when she had said, 'Why don't you just push her?' Push her. And now here she was, giving him grief about coming along on this walk. Like he didn't have enough on his mind.

Summer, for her part, was quiet. She was hard to get a handle on and it seemed for a while, on this hike, that everyone was in his or her own little world. After some time, Hart at least, began to notice it. Like a kid on his first date, he suddenly felt the need to liven things up. He wasn't supposed to be leading some melancholy sheep to slaughter. He had masterminded a well thought out scheme that was designed to astonish. This crime had to have atmosphere. Or at the very least, a lack of tension.

"Ahh," he said loudly, with a smile on his face. "This is great being out here in the great outdoors all al fresco and shit. Excuse my French. Or was that Italian?"

Whatever it was, it didn't illicit much response. "Well, no matter. I just love being out in nature.

It reminds me of when I was a boy scout. Either of you ever in Boy Scouts? No? But I bet you had some boy scouts in you!"

Hart laughed and shook his head. "That one just came together."

"You're a pig," said Brandy.

Well, I guess that would make you a sow, he thought. "There are worse things to be, Brandilita. There are worse things." He said it without offense, determined to keep his mood light.

Hart kept up the talking and sometimes the women would join in. But it was mainly Hart. Despite this, the overall mood had in fact changed and much of the palpable tension was gone.

"I know a great camp spot just on the other side of the bridge," Hart said. "You gonna make it, right Summer?"

She felt her heart banging. "Yeah, yes."

"Sure you can. You conquered it once. You can do it." *Just like falling off a log.*

THIRTY-ONE

UNTIL THEN, THEY HAD generally walked next to each other, but as they got closer to the bridge, Hart began to pull ahead. Then he signaled to Brandy to make sure that she went second and that Summer went last. This was, of course, an important part of the plan.

As Hart took the first step onto the south end of the bridge, his heart really began to rev up. And the women, of course, felt it within themselves as well. You can practice and practice and visualize in your mind until your head aches, but until you get out on the field, you never really know how you're going to perform.

He felt his throat getting dry and he paused for a drink of water. And like an addictive yawn, Summer and Brandy also took a swig. Might as well do something while they waited for Hart to finish his belt.

And then he moved forward, a little too fast, too anxious. About halfway over the bridge he stopped.

And that's when Summer looked down. She had promised herself she wouldn't, but she did. Then she put both hands on the same side of the bridge's railing. Her heart was out of control but her breathing was measured. That much she did remember. However this played out, she'd take it one tiny manageable step at time, piecemeal. And above all, breathe. It would all be over soon.

"Summer," Hart called past Brandy. "I dropped some uh, gloves back there. Black gloves. Would you mind going back and getting them for me? Check by the bushes."

"Sure," she said, instantly turning back toward the south end of the bridge, while Hart and Brandy continued on towards the north end. She walked at a quick pace and right before the last few steps, before stepping off the bridge, she removed her backpack and flung it down on the embankment of the gorge, standing it upright. It took no effort at all to do so as the backpack was filled with very little, and nothing of substantial weight, even though it did appear full.

Next she took out a camcorder, propped it up on top of the backpack, hit the record button and aimed it across the bridge toward Hart and Brandy. Then she reached into some bushes two feet from the head of the bridge. She did all of this very quickly, each step blurring into the next.

By now Hart and Brandy had reached the other end of the bridge and Hart was frantically groping around for his bolt cutters, while Brandy looked on, concerned. Hart had kept his backpack on and Brandy had the tent bag straps over her shoulder as their plan had depended on Summer being lured back across the bridge and they had to keep up appearances. But Summer didn't move.

"Hart," Summer called across the bridge. "What?" he said, not bothering to look up, still beating the bushes, perplexed.

"Looking for this?" Summer held up the bolt cutters.

"Oh my God," said Brandy. She immediately began searching for something. "Where's the rope, Hart?"

"What?" he said. His attention immediately became frantic and divided between what each woman was saying.

"The rope," Brandy said, almost screaming now, and then in a hushed tone out of the side of her mouth, "for reeling up this side of the bridge."

"I moved it. To this side. It's a feng shui thing," Summer called across the bridge.

"Hey, what the fuck is going on?" said Hart, unsure quite yet how to proceed. He waved his arms and began pacing like a caged hyena within an invisible three-foot square.

"Just relax Hart. Try to remain calm." God, it felt great to say that to him after all these years of the shoe being on the other foot. And as if taking her own advice, she did start to feel calm herself. Or at least more wired than scared.

"It's very simple," Summer continued. "You were trying to kill me. Brandy was going to help you and instead I'm stopping you." She felt her voice get stronger with every word.

"You can't beat me, Summer. You're dead." He shook his head. "I got too much riding on this." Then he took a step onto the bridge.

"Hart, wait," said Summer. "Let me tell you what I'm going to do."

Hart stopped and exhaled. "What?"

"Listen, I've got the bolt cutters. I'm going to cut the bridge from my end. You and Brandy hang out on your side for a little while and I'm going to come back with the police."

"Sounds like a shitty plan so far."

"Oh, come on now, Hart, be fair. I never made fun of your plan to kill me. It was pretty solid. Even the old glove routine."

"Yeah well, it's still going to happen. It's just going to be a little sloppy now. But anyway, thanks for telling me your plan."

"Wait a minute, I'm not done."

"Yeah, well hurry up. I want to start collecting on your life insurance."

Two days ago a comment like that would have killed Summer. Now she didn't feel much of anything. Or at least she'd have to feel it later.

"Okay, here are the highlights—I'm going to cut the bridge so I would suggest you're not on it when I do."

"Oh my God! Is she recording this?" It was Brandy. She was pointing to the camcorder.

And then Hart's eyes got very big. He was like a caged bull that was just released as he ran with everything he had across the bridge. But his physical effort was not matching his determination as the load on his back was really slowing him down. He felt forced to cut his speed—almost stop—for a second as he fumbled with his backpack, tossing it haphazardly over the bridge.

This slight break caused him to lose focus on Summer for a moment and he glanced back over his shoulder.

"Come on!" he yelled back to Brandy. "We gotta get to the other side fast!"

Brandy stuttered a second and then started running at top speed, committing to it. Within seconds she hurled the tent she'd been carrying on her shoulder over the side of the bridge as Hart had done with his backpack.

Their movement was quick, slowed now only by the hard and uneven timing of their steps on a bridge not designed for such motion. It caught Summer off guard, for just a moment. She saw the murderous look on Hart's face and immediately crouched down and put the bolt cutters to work, fitting the jaws around one of the ropes that held the bottom of the left side of the bridge. As she gritted her teeth, straining, the idea of not being physically able to make the cut suddenly flashed in her mind for the first time and it horrified her. It took a few seconds of sustained squeezing before the thick rope finally gave way. 'Snip.' One out of four. Her hands ached, but she barely noticed as all she really saw was Hart bearing down on her, mayhem in his eyes.

It scared the hell out of her. And as the bridge shook she could almost feel Hart's hot breath on her neck. Her face exploded with sweat as she grappled with the bolt cutters, trying to reposition herself for the next cut.

Then she heard a shriek. Or maybe more of a war cry. It was Hart. The locomotive was screaming. She had to think fast. She would try to cut the top two ropes, the handrails. They weren't as thick and it should go faster.

As she got up from her squat, her back foot slipped and she kicked her leg out, hitting her backpack, which she felt strike the back of her calf as it fell over. With no time to turn around, she stood up and saw, through her peripheral vision, that the camcorder had been knocked over and along with her backpack, had slid down the lip of the gorge. There went her evidence.

But she couldn't think about that now.

With one side of the bottom "rail" of the bridge now cut, the structure had become even more shaky, making her task harder.

But Hart kept coming, clomping along the right side of the increasingly twisting bridge. And this time she saw that he had a knife in his hand.

Sixty feet away, fifty, forty, thirty. His breath was getting hotter.

She thought about running but instead, like an FBI agent defusing a bomb, she decided to bear down, try to ignore everything else.

This was easier said than done. It was beat the clock and she was torn between focusing on her task at hand and glancing up to see Hart's progress. The idea of being caught off guard terrified her. If she didn't at least pay some attention to him, she could see, in her mind, his boot kicking her in the face any second now while she was staring down at some rope.

'Snip' went one handrail. It was a little easier than the bottom. Certainly faster. Maybe she'd have time for one more. It would have to be the top one. She swung the cutters over to the other side and attempted to position the jaws, trying to time the rhythm of the shaking bridge. She opened them wide and clamped down hard. Glancing up she saw Hart's angry red face. Her eyes remained fixed to his as she squeezed the bolt cutters. 'Snip'. Three out of four and ten feet between them. The last rope wasn't going to happen. So what else could she do with the bolt cutters that would be of any use?

Swinging it above her head, she threw it, like an axe, straight for Hart's head. His shrieking stopped as he backpedaled, his eyes glued to the flying projectile. There wasn't much to hang on to as the handrails, after being cut, had sort of peeled back, hanging limply, while the deck of the bridge was tilting a few degrees to one side, especially near her end of the bridge.

"Move back!" he yelled to Brandy who screamed and took several large steps backward, as did he.

The cutters landed at his feet and he tap danced away so they wouldn't hit him.

"Pick 'em up," he shouted at Brandy as he stepped over them, speeding up again.

Summer's instinct was to scream and run away but she stopped herself. She would not turn her back on him. That was the position of a victim and she knew if she assumed it, it would affect her whole psyche. If that happened it would be all over for her.

So instead she moved forward, her steps deliberate. After quickly removing her sweat suit jacket, she grounded herself as best she could on the increasingly unstable bridge. Staring into Hart's eyes, she continued her advance. She could feel the terror in her face and wondered if Hart had picked up on it. She wanted to cry and knew she would—but later.

Hart was taken aback for a moment and stopped. Then he clenched his knife and held it a little higher and smiled.

Then not to be outdone by his gesture of confidence, she said, "Okay okay, Hart, I'll bring you the gloves you asked for. Calm down."

Hart scoffed and continued walking toward her, his knife held a little in front of him.

When they were within striking distance of each other, Summer held her hands up near her face, open palmed and then swung her right hand toward Hart's head. The punch was pulled but had served its purpose. As Hart watched her hands, he didn't realize that she had pivoted her body and then quickly struck his hand with a middle swinging kick which knocked his knife into the air. Hanging there for a moment it dropped like a stone into the belly of the gorge below.

Everyone was surprised—even Summer.

"I guess karate lessons have paid off," he blurted out, not allowing himself to indicate that his hand had been injured by her kick.

Summer felt emboldened but uneasy by her position on the bridge. She had to move things more toward the center where the bridge was more stable as it was closer to the uncut north end.

Charging forward, her hands moved quickly as she threw multiple straight punches—mainly in the air—as she had practiced numerous times in her karate classes. It took Hart off-guard and he quickly backpedaled. Brandy put her hands out to avoid being steamrolled and backpedaled herself, one step behind Hart.

And then in the midst of the punches, Summer surprised him with a front kick to his shin which caused him to stumble. Coming out of it, he charged forward, locking his hands around her throat. She instinctively tried to pry his hands away but he was too strong for her. Then he pulled his right hand back and struck her in the face, a hard but glancing blow. She felt dazed and wondered if she might pass out.

"Yeah! Get her," Brandy said through clenched teeth, shaking her fists.

Summer's face felt hot where Hart had struck her and she imagined a huge welt on her cheek. He pulled back again just as she was about to kick him. But he was too fast for her and the blow completely neutralized her kick as it just fizzled in the air.

Brandy danced behind him throwing air punches like she was watching a heavyweight fight on T.V. and her hometown boy had just turned the tide.

It appeared that Hart had found a winning strategy and he cocked his fist back again. But doing the same thing over and over again in war is rarely a winning strategy. It's like telegraphing your punches to a boxer and sooner or later you pay for it. For Hart it would be sooner. The moment his fingers left her throat this time, Summer's hands jetted outward as she planted a thumb in each of his eyes. And as he moved backward, Summer moved forward, her energy culminating in a tremendous front kick to Hart's ribs.

She knew she had hurt him the moment her foot hit him, and her hands instinctively went up near the front of her face as she watched him fall.

And then came the cry of pain. Not from Hart, but from Brandy.

The speed of Summer's kick had taken everyone off guard and as Hart had toppled backward he landed on top of a scrambling Brandy who had been trying to turn and run. Her foot, in a starting block position, took the full brunt of Hart's dead weight, twisting and cracking her ankle on impact.

Hart rolled a little to the side to free Brandy's foot. But despite this movement, it was clear from the excruciating look on his face that he wouldn't be getting up too quickly.

They were at about mid-bridge at this point and the swaying was getting worse and for a moment Hart and Summer just looked at each other. They were both out of breath. She wanted to ask him 'why?' but she restrained herself, not wanting to hear some smug answer.

It was Hart's eyes that first broke contact as they drifted downward to something he hadn't really absorbed before this—not since Summer had removed her sweat suit jacket. Running vertically down Summer's chest were two straps connected by one horizontal strap. *I thought her backpack was off.* And he envisioned her suddenly reaching back like a samurai and pulling out a sword.

But instead she turned her back to him and began heading back to the south end of the bridge.

"Give me the cutters. Quick, quick," Hart said to Brandy, who was wailing in pain. He slapped at her leg with great impatience until she passed them to him.

"Wait," he yelled to Summer. She turned around.

Hart looked down. "Help me. Please," he said, barely able to get out the words.

Summer sighed. "That's what I'm doing, Hart. I'm going to get the police. They'll get you off of here."

She only hoped they'd believe her. After all, she'd been the one to cut the bridge, Hart's confession was gone and it would be two against one. Maybe getting the police wasn't such a great idea after all.

"No. No cops. Help me off this bridge or I swear I'll cut this last rope." He had positioned the cutters and was holding the handles at the ready.

"No!" Brandy screamed as she began to drag herself toward the north end of the bridge.

"Shut up, Brandy!" he shouted, looking over his shoulder. The simple act of turning around and then back again made him wince in pain. "I'm not kidding, Summer. If I die, you die."

"Hart," she shook her head. "You can't hurt me anymore."

"Don't test me, Summer. I got nothing to lose."

By now Brandy had gotten herself onto her one good foot and began to hobble her way toward the end of the bridge.

Summer turned around again and began walking away. "Stop talking and do what you have to do, Hart."

"Dammit," he said, rubbing his face.

"Don't do it Hart! Don't do it!" Brandy wailed over her shoulder, hopping on one foot, trying to speed up.

Hart squeezed the cutters slowly hoping Summer would feel the collapsing bridge and know he meant business. If she did feel anything, she didn't react.

He was about to give it a final squeeze when the bridge gave way, the final rope unable to do the job of all the supports anymore.

As the rope snapped, gravity took over. Brandy tried to scream but anything audible that was there caught in her throat as the north half of the bridge went pummeling toward the wall of the gorge.

She wasn't sure what was worse, falling straight down to her certain death or crashing into the side of the gorge and then falling to her certain death. Unable to think clearly, by pure instinct, she squeezed whatever rope she could wrap her hands around and held on for all she could.

She clenched her teeth and right before hitting this natural edifice, an image flashed in her mind of her holding on and using the bridge like a ladder that would carry her to safety. But that idea was smashed, along with her body, as she drove, like a human wrecking ball, into the great wall of the gorge and was subsequently flicked away.

And even though Hart had contributed greatly to knocking over that last domino, he couldn't help being taken off guard. It felt like a trap door had been triggered and the effect was instant and terrifying. The ultimate helplessness. He was moving faster than he could comprehend. He looked down and to the side and finally up. And that's when he saw it. The sky was being blocked out by a big green canopy. And just below it was Summer. And she was yelling.

"Is this enough dramatic flair for you, Hart?"

He probably didn't hear her but it sure felt good to say it.

THIRTY-TWO

SUMMER WOULDN'T HAVE much time. In what would seem like a counterintuitive move under any other circumstance, she pulled on the toggles and was actually trying to steer her parachute into—or more technically, toward—the south wall of the gorge. If she could pull this off it would save her an innumerable amount of time and heartache.

She had two things going for her. She had put her hand on the ripcord right after her last conversation with Hart and her reflexes in pulling it without much delay— whether out of skill or fear— had been excellent.

The second fortunate thing was that she had been moving down the bridge in the right direction, toward the south wall, when the final rope had given way. As a result she was almost directly over her target when she had yanked the cord.

Her idea was to grab onto the rope that was now hanging down from the tree that she had tied it to when she had switched things up on Hart. If things had gone according to her original plan, she would have gotten Hart and Brandy's confession on tape and cut the bridge when they had been on the north end of the gorge. Then she would have returned with the police and they would have used the rope that was tied to the tree to reel up the bridge.

The rope in question, that was now hanging down the south end of the gorge, was close to two hundred feet long and had now taken the form of a giant loop.

This brainstorm was all improvisation of course. Other than having the foresight to put on a parachute container under her sweat suit jacket, the way everything had unfolded would have been impossible to have planned out and if this didn't work, she would have had to have found a way back up the gorge from the bottom.

At a certain point Summer could no longer steer as she needed both hands to grab the rope, so she was forced to let go of the steering toggles.

When she finally did grab the rope she was about ten feet from the bottom of the loop and while the parachute slowed her down she was still moving pretty quickly. Forced to slide down the rope, as the parachute descended, was painful and she was scared of losing the skin on her hands. In order to slow down more, she wrapped her legs around the rope. At least her pants would protect her somewhat. This turned out to be a good move because as she slid downward, she simply guided her feet into the bottom of the loop. Then she bent her legs slowly and came to a relatively gradual stop.

By this time Summer was drenched in sweat. As she looked down into the gorge as far as she could, she was grateful that she was up here.

Using the rope and the natural texture of the walls in front of her, Summer took her time as she scaled what was just another hurdle. Back on top again.

EPILOGUE

The top of the newspaper read:

The Local Buzz
Cardsdale, CA
Circulation 438

It had a graphic of a bee next to the word 'Buzz'. Summer sat with perfect posture at her desk. She studied the insect for a moment before allowing her eyes to drift downward to the headline. It blared with excitement:

CORRECTION: HUSBAND AND WIFE'S *COUSIN* DIE IN FIERY EXPLOSION

It had been the biggest story to hit Cardsdale since Huncke's stopped serving homemade pie.

Summer scanned down the page when she felt a pair of hands rest on her neck. Hart's face flashed in her mind and without hesitation she dropped the newspaper, seized the intruding fingers, whirled around and pinned them behind the offender's back in one fluid motion.

"Okay, okay, take it easy. I give up," he said.

"Oh, Mr. Day. It's you," said Summer releasing Bob's fingers. He spun around and embraced her.

"I asked you not to call me that, Mrs. Day," he said, his lips moving close to hers.

"Sorry," she said, in between kisses. "Old habits die hard."

"Mommy! Mommy!" the two girls yelled as they skidded into the room, breaking Bob and Summer's embrace like bowling balls rolling into a couple of pins.

"And?" said Bob, feigning anger.

They both screamed out *Daddy!* and everyone hugged everyone goodnight.

"Now off to bed now. It's getting late. I'll tuck you girls in, in a minute."

The girls ran giggling off as the couple drifted back into each other's arms.

"Coming to bed?" Bob asked.

"Soon. I just have a few briefs to look over first."

"Can't it wait 'til tomorrow?"

Summer kept one arm around Bob's waist as she nudged the yellowing newspaper out of the way and reached for a file on her desk.

"See this?" she asked, with a good-natured twinkle.

The file read *Day and Day Attorneys at Law.*

"Alright, I get you."

They hugged again and exchanged kisses, before he turned and headed toward the door.

"Goodnight, Counselor."

"Goodnight, Counselor."

"Hey, Bob."

"Yeah, Sweetheart," he said turning his head.

"You ever regret making me a partner?"

He smiled. "Not on any level."

LUCKY STEVENS'

The Pull Out Method

IS NOW AVAILABLE ON AMAZON.COM

Turn the page for a sneak preview…

THE TIMING, DEPENDING on how you look at it, was perfect. They entered just like anyone else, and no one paid any attention to them at all. Two men dressed in brown UPX uniforms, hauling boxes, generally don't raise too many eyebrows. Both men wore dark sunglasses, which was pretty normal, considering the blazing sun outside, and both sported full goatees.

The shorter of the two approached the security guard, who looked like a walking cliché. He was about seventy years old or so, and looked as though he'd have trouble guarding his own breakfast. The shorter man mumbled something inaudible to him, which made the guard chuckle. Now that had to be a courtesy chuckle, the man thought to himself. Even I don't know what I said.

By now, the taller of the two men decked out in United Parcel X-press uniforms was bending down and tying his shoe a few feet behind the guard. The first man looked at the guard and repeated his gibberish as if expecting an answer.

The guard squinted and, getting the feeling that more than just a chuckle was required of him, craned his neck forward, turning his head in the process. By then it was too late. The guard's tie was securely clenched in the man's strong grip, and the taller man had already bounded over and removed the guard's gun from its holster. With their free hands, both men reached under their caps, grabbed their sunglasses, and pulled ski masks over their faces, both of their "goatees" dropping to the floor as they did so. They then replaced their sunglasses back over their masks.

"On the floor, Pops," the taller man, Duke, said to the guard, giving him a little nudge. Then he fired the guard's gun into the ceiling while the shorter man, Bobby, ran over to the doors and wrapped a cable and padlock around the handles.

"Everybody get down on the floor!" yelled Duke, his voice loud and gravelly.

"Down on the floor," repeated Bobby, brandishing his own weapon, a nine millimeter.

Both men pointed their guns around the room. And as if it had been rehearsed, the screams, whimpering, and uncontrollable sobbing began immediately. "And just so there aren't any misunderstandings, yes, this is a bank robbery. Now the good news is, we just need some walking-around money. The bad news is, we do *a lot* of walking," said Duke.

Fran McDougal, a veteran teller, was shivering, her finger hovering around the silent alarm button before finally pushing it.

Duke's eyes were on fire as he zeroed in on a closed office door toward the back of the bank. The sign on the door read, "George Sullivan Bank Manager."

"George!" bellowed Duke as he stomped toward the door, thrusting it open. George Sullivan was cowering in the corner, his arms moving up and down in front of his face like a flinchy boxer.

"I'm sorry, I thought you said, 'Come in,'" said Duke. "Come on, George." He grabbed the back of George's neck and led him out, back into the main lobby. "Or do you prefer Mr. Sullivan?" George's lips were moving, but nothing was coming out. "Whatsa matter? You act like this is your first robbery. Get over there." Duke pointed to the floor, near some other hostages.

By now, Bobby had placed thick black bags over all the security cameras that he could reach and had spray-painted over the lenses of those he couldn't reach. "Now, what the hell is this ladder doing here?" asked Duke. "Don't you people know this is dangerous?" And then to Bobby: "Number Two, get everyone into a circle over there, around the corner, near Mr. Sullivan's office. Take care of their cell phones." Duke looked at the orange fiberglass ladder. "Gonzalez A/C" was written down its side. Then he looked up at the opening in the ceiling.

"I need all employees of Gonzalez A/C to get their asses down here!"

ONE

WHEN LIFE GIVES YOU SHIT, make lemonade. Never in my life would I need those words more than last Sunday. Especially as I was on my way to see her. Hard to believe at the time, but she would almost be the least of my problems.

She was a wild girl. Lulu. Absolutely balls-to-the- wall crazy and fun. And she excited me to no end. Hell, I was only eighteen years old when we had met and I'd been running with the bottom end of the lineup by then for a good three years. I saw no end in sight, a false sense of invincibility having snuffed out what little common sense I had at the time.

At nineteen I joined the army.

"What're you nuts, baby?" I remember my grandma saying at the time. Then again, that's what she said about my going out with the previously mentioned her, too. I guess at the time, I didn't care what anybody said. You see, those were the good old days—when I knew everything.

Anyway, I joined the army. It seemed like the thing to do. And all throughout those four miserable, yet fairly educational, years, Lulu and I were going strong, or so I thought.

Yeah, that was the life, all right. Free room and board and weekend furloughs. And of course, the drinking, drugs, and small petty crimes. It must have been fun, because I don't remember it that well.

All that changed, though, on February 22, 2007. That's the day Trevor was born, and the day I decided to try to be a better person. It didn't even occur to me until a few years later that he might not actually even be mine. But by then, it didn't matter. I saw his tiny face, little fingers, and curly hair, and I guess I was hooked.

Now, when I said that everything changed that day, I need to be more clear. It was more like the beginning of a change. One that would come slowly and, I guess I hate to say, still seems to be going on. That's me. Lulu is, and was, a different story.

She hadn't changed a bit after Trevor was born. I guess I was a little surprised, but couldn't really blame her. I mean, I was "smart" enough to pick her, right? And she was *exactly* what the outside wrapping advertised—a crazy, stupid, out-of-control train wreck waiting to happen. In other words, everything I had been on February 21, 2007.

Anyway, these were the thoughts that rolled around in my mind as I drove down Laurel Canyon toward her apartment on Highlander Street. Now I'm going to be completely honest with you. At that moment, I still hadn't totally adjusted to the idea of being a father. I mean, I always loved my son, but, I don't know, I guess the responsible, "picket fence" lifestyle is what was tripping me up.

In any event, things were happening that suggested I better quickly get used to the idea of fatherhood and all it entailed. It was Sunday, and the next day was my hearing in front of a judge in downtown L.A. Depending on what his decision was, Trevor could be coming to live with me full-time.

I'm actually the one who set off this legal action and even my lawyer didn't give me much of a chance. I've seen *Kramer vs. Kramer*. The system almost always favors the mother. But I had to do it. I just didn't like the way my ex was doing things— nothing terrible, or so I thought, but I just knew Trevor deserved more. And it didn't take long for me to realize I knew I was doing the right thing.

It all started when I first mentioned to Lulu that I'd like to spend more time with Trevor. For $100,000 to cover "child support," I could keep him permanently, she said. And I guess as her idea of a bonus, neither one of us would ever see her again. Her bizarre twisting of the term "child support" aside, her meaning came in loud and clear. I filed for custody the next day.

So why head over to her apartment? All I can say is that morning when I woke up, I felt strange. Empty. I had a bad feeling about it, and I kept telling myself that the hearing was tomorrow. Just wait and see what happens. But I couldn't. An overwhelming desire came over me like I just had to see my son. The anticipation gnawed at the back of my brain.

I started thinking about my ex and how nicely she can put herself together when she wants to. I thought about the great front she can put up. A born actress. And for the first time since this whole thing began, I thought about the $100,000. I thought maybe it would just be better to give her the money. Make a clean break and start all over. I guess the fact that I was about $99,000 light didn't really occur to me at that moment in time. And the idea of avoiding a courtroom certainly appealed to me as well, having never had a good experience in any of the courtrooms I'd ever been in.

As I turned right onto Highlander, my stomach dropped. I had only been there once before, and that was at night. The sun hung in the sky like an over-watted light bulb, shining brightly as the cockroaches dove for cover. Only these cockroaches weren't going anywhere. They felt too at home among the abandoned cars, appliances, and skin-and-bone mattresses that decorated the trashy sidewalks and curbs of this semi-suburban Beirut. The cover of night did this place justice.

As I turned my head from the filth of the sidewalks back to the filth of the street, I suddenly slammed on my brakes, barely missing a gang of young boys who had bolted out of nowhere to cross right in front of my car. They were completely unfazed by the screeching of my tires, floating by like crashing waves. They seemed to almost bounce off of each other in different directions, but yet they somehow seemed to be all gummed together. The small stack of books that sat on the passenger side of the front seat weren't so lucky, as they scattered in all directions—Fitzgerald, Faulkner, and Orwell one way, Steinbeck and Dr. Seuss, another.

I exhaled loudly, stopping long enough for my body to collapse within itself. I let my head drop, totally aware of the fact that my foot was firmly on the brake. And when I finally looked up, I couldn't believe what I was seeing was real. It was Trevor.

He was playing, by himself, about ten yards from my car. My immediate reaction was visceral, angry. But my brain took over and I decided to be calm, take it in, and try not to overreact.

I looked around. He was definitely alone. Completely unsupervised. Three and a half years old. *Three and a half years old!* my brain screamed. My son. Filthy and playing in garbage, in nothing more than a diaper and a thin white t-shirt. Staying calm suddenly seemed a lot harder.

But for his sake, I did stay calm. The last thing I wanted to do was freak him out. I prayed there was some kind of misunderstanding, but certainly couldn't fathom what it could be.

After I parked the car, I approached my son. "Trev—" I said softly, this single word catching as my throat closed. It caught me off guard. It felt so surreal. Literally not being able to speak.

He immediately broke from his trance, and from the little song he was singing. His mouth opened wide and curled into a broad smile.

"Daddy!" he yelled. He scrambled to his feet, and we ran toward each other. I held him so tightly, I was almost scared I'd hurt him. I didn't want to let go. I was still afraid I wouldn't be able to talk yet, as puddles collected on my lower eyelids.

I was strangely aware of my gathering tears and dreaded that inevitable first blink that would squeeze them out and send them rolling down my cheeks.

"Why you're crying, Daddy?"

I laughed, as I thought about how his question was filled with such an unaware innocence. And how his words made me want to cry even harder.

"I'm just so happy to see you, Trevor." My voice shivered and cracked, but I had gotten the words out.

As I climbed the stairs to Lulu's apartment, Trevor's grip around my neck seemed to tighten. He began to shake, and a feeling of anxiousness washed over me. I'd have to think of something else; this wasn't the time to confront her. I turned to go back down.

"I want my teddy bear, Daddy."

"Where is it?" I said. I tried to sound calm. "In Mommy's house."

I sighed. "We're gonna have to get it later, Trevor. I'm sorry."

He began to cry softly as I walked down the stairs. By the time I had reached the last step, his shaking had almost stopped. His grip around my neck was looser. Leaving was a good idea, and I headed toward my car.

"Reggie."

The voice was unfamiliar.

I turned around and saw a woman in her late sixties, early seventies. She had a face that looked like she'd worked hard all her life and really had nothing to show for it. But still, there was a sweetness to it. She wore a flower print dress that for some reason caught my eye during those first few seconds when you sum someone up.

"Yes?" I said. Despite her, uh, harmlessness, I felt on guard. I guess it was the circumstances.

"Do you remember me?" she asked.

The See's Candy lady flashed in my mind. My anxiety intensified. I really didn't want to take any walks down memory lane. Not now.

"We weren't in the same kindergarten together, were we?" I don't know why I said it, but I did. I hoped it didn't sound snotty or sarcastic.

Fortunately, she laughed. "I'm Mrs. Haynes."

"Oh, oh yeah, I remember you. You used to babysit me every once in a while."

"Right, right. And you know I'm still friends with your grandma."

I smiled. "Mrs. Haynes, could you do me a favor?" Lulu's apartment door was halfway open. I opened it the rest of way with my purposely careless knock. I expected it to be messy, but the place was a pigsty. A lot worse than I thought it would be. But then again, Lulu could always clean up pretty good, I mean *well*, when she wanted to. Like if she had known I was coming, for example, you wouldn't have recognized the place. It was part of what worried me about facing her in court, the next day. Unlike that moment, the next day, she wouldn't be surprised. With a little advanced warning, she really knows how to put on a show.

Her head, which was resting soundly on the couch, seemed to percolate upward as her glassy eyes scanned for familiarity. She wore a t-shirt whose hem—if that's what it's called—landed just below her navel. Beneath that was a pair of white cotton panties, and nothing else. I hate to admit it, but she still turned me on.

"Reggie?"

I completely ignored my unwilling and sick attraction to her, and with Trevor safely in Mrs. Haynes' care, I let loose.

"What the fuck do you think you're doing?" I said. My mouth barely opened, due to the fact that I couldn't seem to stop clenching my teeth.

"What? Whuz with you?" she slurred as she casually stumbled down the hall. I followed. I could smell the alcohol on her breath.

When she reached the end of the hall, she stepped through the door, pulled down her panties, and backed her way onto the toilet. Over the gushing sound of Niagara Falls, I continued.

"Do you know that I just found Trevor outside by himself playing in a pile of filth right by the street?"

"Who?" she slurred. "Trevor! Our son!"

She laughed. "I know, I know who yer talkin' about. I'm just kidding…God."

I could feel the sweat puddling on the back of my neck. I wanted to kill her. I won't lie, I wanted to wrap my hands around her throat and just squeeze the demented life out of her.

Instead, I took a deep breath and let it out slowly. By now, Lulu had finished in the bathroom. Quite the environmentalist, too. I guess flushing the toilet and washing your hands wastes a little too much water.

"All right. I'm taking Trevor and I'll see you in court tomorrow," I said.

"Whatya' mean you're taking him? I got legal cus'ody."

I took out my phone and began taking pictures of her apartment. "Not after tomorrow you won't."

"Oh fuck you. Those pictures don't mean shit," she said. She seemed to be sobering up. "Besides, you got two strikes on you. You're not getting no cus'ody."

I kept on taking pictures—of the dirty dishes, the clothes all over the floor, the trash, the half-eaten food, the alcohol bottles, and even the primarily empty refrigerator— as if I hadn't heard her. But I had heard her, and she was right. I do have two strikes. And for those of you who don't know, in California, after your third strike, or y'know, felony, in other words, you go to jail for life. Ironically, as a father who wants a safer world for his son, I think it's a pretty good law, but uh, anyway, here we are.

I'm not proud of my crimes, and to be honest, like all ex-cons, I should have more than two strikes. After all, you only get those strikes when you're caught.

Not that it's an excuse, but most of what I did, I did when I was young—not to mention stupid. Stealing cars, mainly. That's when I first got pinched, as an adult that is. My juvenile record had been expunged and I decided to celebrate by stealing a cop's car. Only I didn't know it was a cop's car. The judge didn't seem to care. I got a year in prison for that one. I was a regular Einstein all right.

I guess I didn't get the message, because after I got out, I continued stealing cars, before and *during* my army years. I never got caught again for it though, so I guess I did learn something.

The last thing I got in trouble for, was for something completely different. It also has a bit of irony to it. It was actually the only violent offense I ever committed. Up until then, I had never even seen any of my victims. Not that this guy was exactly a victim.

What happened was, one night me and Lulu— I mean Lulu and *I*—were in a bar having a few beers when something happened, I don't remember what, but anyway, this guy starts saying he's going to kill Lulu. At first I thought he was kidding, but he starts getting angrier and angrier, and I really looked at him and realized he was serious. Next thing I know he pulls out a knife and lunges with it, at Lulu. Then he and I started really brawling. He got in a couple good shots, but it ended when I broke his jaw. They never found the knife, and I guess he must have looked worse than I did, because he got three months and I got eight. Strike two.

What made it ironic was that I got my second strike saving Lulu's life so that five years later she could use that second strike against me to try to get custody of our son who wouldn't even be here today if I hadn't saved her life. Anyway, when she mentioned the two strikes, I guess my face gave me away, and like any successful leech, Lulu seemed to smell blood.

"You know if you'd just give me the child support— the hundred thou—this would all be over," she said, as if I could just write her a check.

"Where the hell am I going to get a hundred thousand dollars?"

She shrugged. "That's your problem. Do watcha' gotta do."

"As always Lulu, it's been a little slice of heaven." I turned toward the door.

"See you in court," she said.

When I reached the door, I almost collided with this wiry-looking guy with no front teeth who was on his way in. Without making eye contact, he swerved around me and planted himself inside the apartment.

"Hey, Lulu," he said. He tried to sound sexy but failed.

"Hey, Chucky," she said. "Wait in the bedroom, baby."

I was only a few feet out the door when she called my name. I turned around.

She was holding up two fingers. "Two strikes," she said, smiling. "Keep your eye on the ball."

I could feel my nostrils flare as I turned and walked directly toward her. She looked a little surprised, then stuck her chest out defiantly.

"Go ahead, hit me. With a black eye in court tomorrow, your case would look even worse than it does now."

With the back of my hand, I nudged her to the side as I re-entered her apartment.

"If I was going to hit you, it'd be in the stomach, where it wouldn't leave a mark."

Then I began to poke around the apartment. "Well, get out of here already. I got company.

What're you doing?"

I reached down behind the television and grabbed a little beige teddy bear.

"Got it," I said, as I walked past her, and out the door.

"Hey, Reggie!" she called after me. "When I'm done in here, Trevor better be out there or there's gonna be trouble, asshole."

As soon as Trevor was securely fastened in the back seat of my car, we began to roll, and I really began to think. Every few moments, I'd glance up into the rearview mirror just to look at him. He was sitting quietly, holding his teddy bear in one hand and a book in the other. What a great kid. Maybe I was asking for trouble. I mean, he was technically in her custody, and I was taking off with him, with my hearing the next day. And here I am trying to be a better person. I mean, I didn't feel guilty, but I knew it wouldn't look good in court. But I guess the bottom line was, I just knew I had to get Trevor out of that dangerous situation.

I decided to call my grandma and then my lawyer— in that order. My grandma is the greatest woman I've ever known, flat out. To me, no one is smarter or tougher. I was lucky enough to be raised by her.

Now I know some of you out there are probably thinking that she didn't do a very good job with me from what I've told you so far. And I can understand people thinking that, but I'll tell you, anything bad I've done in my life has been my fault, a hundred percent. I take full responsibility. My grandma did everything right as far as I'm concerned. Some people, no matter what, are just too stupid to listen. That was me. "Just because the milk comes out of the cow spoiled, doesn't mean it's the farmer's fault—or the cow's." That was one of her little sayings. One of hundreds, I'm guessing, and it seems to be appropriate here. "You should write a book," I used to always tell her.

Another thing I always admired about my grandma was her toughness. She was raised in the South, and her father insisted she always carry a gun. When she was in her late teens, she shot and killed a man who tried to rape her sister. She was finally acquitted in an unnecessarily long and traumatic trial. "What does a mother lioness protecting her cubs know about man-made laws? And what does she care? It's instinct, and I'd do it all again, even if they had strung me up for it." That's how she always used to end that story.

"Now Grams, no matter what happens, you know nothing about me taking Tr—I mean, uh, my progeny. As far as you're concerned, it was my weekend. You're not getting in trouble over this," I told my grandma over the phone as I drove.

"Baby," she said, "we really gotta talk."

"I know. We will. I already have a few ideas. But for now, listen, please. *She* knows where both of us live. So, I'll meet you at the Van Nuys Glen Motel on Van Nuys and Chandler. Now when you get there—hold on." It was my call waiting. Mr. Gonzalez. "Grams, I gotta take this. I'll see you soon." I clicked over.

"Yes, Mr. Gonzalez." I listened to him talk and, under the circumstances, knew I didn't have a choice. "Yeah, I got it. San Fernando Bank and Trust. I'll be there."

Lucky Stevens' skill as a writer extends far beyond the text of this novel. He also wrote the dedication, the acknowledgments page, and the very words you are reading right now at this exact second. *Keep Calm and Kill Your Wife* is his second and, some say, greatest novel to date.

Lucky can be contacted at:
luckystevenswriter@gmail.com